THE DEATH MISER

John Creasey

Master crime fiction writer John Creasey's 562 titles have sold more than 80 million copies in over 25 languages. After enduring 743 rejection slips, the young Creasey's career was kickstarted by winning a newspaper writing competition. He went on to collect multiple honours from The Mystery Writers of America including the Edgar Award for best novel in 1962 and the coveted title of Grand Master in 1969. Creasey's prolific output included 11 different series including Roger West, the Toff, the Baron, Patrick Dawlish, Gideon, Dr Palfrey, and Department Z, published both under his own name and 10 other pseudonyms.

Creasey was born in Surrey in 1908 and, when not travelling extensively, lived between Bournemouth and Salisbury for most of his life. He died in England in 1973.

THE DEPARTMENT Z SERIES

THE DEATH MISER

JOHN CREASEY

ipso books

This edition published in 2016 by Ipso Books

First published in Great Britain by Melrose in 1933

Ipso Books is a division of Peters Fraser + Dunlop Ltd

Drury House, 34-43 Russell Street, London WC2B 5HA

Copyright © John Creasey, 1933, revised edition, 1965

CONTENTS

1

Concerning a Dog and some Others

TWO large hands, which were the exclusive property of the Hon. James Quinion, cupped themselves gently round the small, smooth-skinned face of Lady Gloria Runsey. Two humorous and quizzical eyes matched their speckled grey with hers.

'My dear aunt,' said the Hon. James. 'In the last hour at least two more wrinkles have grown on your forehead. It's a positive and unforgivable sin, and if you let it happen again I shall rate you a square forever.'

Lady Gloria laughed.

She was sitting in a deep arm-chair by the open French windows of Runsey Hall, whilst the lazy warmth of a late September sun lulled the aching of her frail body. For many years she had sat in the chair by the window when the weather had been kind, looking at the world in which she had been wont to wander willy-nilly before paralysis had robbed her legs of their strength and made her a captive. She had spent those years cheerfully, and much of her near-happiness she owed to the laughing, carefree nephew who now stood over her.

Quinion took an Egyptian cigarette from a gold case and lit it with great care. He was a vast man, uncommonly broad of shoulder and long of limb, but his clothes—at the moment he wore a suit of silver greys—fitted him too perfectly. They spoke of affectation, and the perfumed cigarettes, the scented oil that he used for his hair and the complete correctness of every small item of his everyday apparel bespoke the dandy. In a small man these things might have passed unnoticed, but in the huge Quinion they were incongruous to a point of repulsion.

Of these things Lady Gloria Runsey had been thinking and talking for the past hour, and her companion had been Colonel Cann, a fact which James Quinion had noticed without approval. Colonel Cann, a man's man and no nonsense, held harshly unpleasant views on Quinion, and considered that his—the colonel's—sister was all kinds of a fool for putting up with him; in fact, he believed she encouraged him. Quinion tweaked her ear lightly, pulled a hassock to her feet and, squatting on it, spoke with little respect for his uncle.

'I take it that the great Colonel Damn has been blasting me. I don't think that he would think life worth living if he couldn't slate me once a day and twice on Sundays. What's his latest effort? Or does he think I'm beyond redemption?'

Once again Lady Gloria laughed. This utter absurdity of Jimmy's was infectious; a man who could make a butt for humour of his own habits and discuss his faults with such complete *applomb* was surely less of a fool than he looked. Only—Lady Gloria sighed mentally—why *did* he make himself look such a fool?

Quinion went on.

'If it would please him, of course, I could pop over-
seas and pot some lions, or drive a hovercraft, or spend
six months in Moscow. Or he might like me to enter the
world of commerce, or adopt a cause in the name of action.
All of which things might appeal to some people, but they
leave me stone cold; in fact, they leave me freezing.' He was
laughing now, and his firm white teeth gleamed between his
masculine lips, creating the appearance of a man who was a
man. His sizeable jaw swept round masterfully, ending in a
cleft chin which added to the impression of strength already
lent to his countenance by clear eyes and healthily tanned
skin.

'I think,' she said slowly, 'that he would be satisfied if
you didn't look quite so . . . useless . . . sometimes.' She eyed
her companion squarely, refusing to respond to his laughter. 'You do slide through life, don't you, Jimmy?'

Quinion stood up, tossing the Egyptian cigarette
through the open window and watching the spiral of smoke
which curled lazily upwards, losing itself in the deep blue of
the sky.

'Life,' he said finally, looking straight at Lady Gloria, 'is
taken far too seriously. I have youth, money and the gift of
fair words; with them I can take things easily and enjoy living. All the Colonel Damns in the world wouldn't make me
take up a career. Apart from that, there is a suggestion in
the air that I'm not capable of looking after myself'—his
expression was half serious and half humorous, revealing
a side of his nature at which Lady Gloria had only guessed
before— 'and, if it weren't for the fact that I rather like the
dear old Colonel Damn, I'd resent that suggestion. You see'
—he pressed her thin fingers between his own, and the tone
of his voice became strangely purposeful— 'it doesn't do to
put all your cards on the table . . . and things are not always

what they seem.' He grinned again, slipping back into his old, familiar, inconsequential manner. 'Satisfied?'

Lady Gloria Runsey nodded slowly, half-smiling.

'I wish I knew where you go for your holidays, Jimmy.'

Quinion placed one large hand beneath her chin, and shook the other half an inch from her nose.

'If you're very good I might tell you some day,' he said. 'Live in hope.'

An hour later a large-limbed, clear-eyed young man strode rapidly across the Sussex Downs from the direction of Runsey Hall towards Runsey village. He was clad in a disreputable sports jacket, a pair of flannels that would have disgraced an under-gardener, down-at-heel brogues and an open-necked shirt. Between his firm, white teeth he gripped an old and much-charred pipe, and in spite of the fact that he had taken a cold shower less than twenty minutes before, his dark, wavy hair was bared to the cool breezes of the Downs.

Many folks would have commented on the likeness between the young man and the Hon. James Quinion; few would have believed that it was Quinion himself; none the less, it was.

He was looking ahead as he walked, and appeared to be thinking with far more concentration than most people gave him credit for. He possessed many traits which were not generally known. He was, in fact, thinking of a telegram which he had received an hour before.

Telegrams of similar nature had often come to him during the four preceding years, and directly after them he had taken a holiday from England, and spent a week, a month, or even longer in what Colonel Cann described as 'women, wine and perdition'. Colonel Cann would have been a much surprised man had he known that those frequent 'holidays' had been spent in working for an organization which even the most confirmed fighting man held in considerable awe, and which the man in the street knew of, vaguely, as the Secret Service. Life with Quinion was certainly seldom exactly what it seemed.

For the first time, however, the telegram had given instructions which would keep him in England; it was this which puzzled him as he turned the wording of it over in his mind.

Watch Thomas Loder Cross Farm near Runsey report daily and give names of visitors.

Even as he had decoded it, he had wondered on its wisdom. 'It's all right so far as it goes,' he had reflected, 'but it's very close to home.' Then he had shrugged his shoulders; after all, the people at head-quarters knew their business.

He knew Cross Farm. It was a small place with a rambling and unkempt farmhouse which had been empty for years before Thomas Loder, the man of the telegram, had leased it and lived in it. Loder had been in the neighbourhood for six months, but Quinion had never set eyes on him; the newcomer kept himself very much to himself.

A sudden sound made the Hon. James stop in his tracks and strain his ears to catch a repetition. It was the combination of a bark, a snarl and a whimper, and it came from behind a small clump of bushes fifty yards to his right. Quickly upon it came the unmistakable voice of a man raised in that objectionable type of anger which finds expression in obscenity, and a swishing sound as of a whip cutting through the air; a yelp and a pitiful whimpering followed. Quinion broke into a run towards the bushes.

Before he had sighted the man and the dog yet another voice reached his ears. Coming from some distance it was obviously a woman's, and Jimmy caught the words: 'Peter . . . Peter . . . come here, boy. . . .'

There's a woman there, thought Quinion, rounding the bushes. He came suddenly upon the man and the dog.

The former looked round, his whip poised in the air.

'Drop it,' said Quinion.

The man brought the whip down cruelly upon the quivering body of the dog, a large Alsatian whose coat showed a number of livid weals. Its eyes turned towards Jimmy in piteous entreaty; the spirit was beaten out of him and he was too weak to show any fight.

In two strides Quinion was in front of the heavily-built, swarthy-faced man whose smallish eyes were blazing. The whip was suddenly snatched from his hand and sent flying into the clump of bushes. The man cursed, made as though to lunge at Quinion and then kicked viciously at the dog. Quinion's leg shot out, locked for a moment in the other's and then jerked upwards; thirteen stone of flesh and bone turned a half-somersault in the air and the man landed heavily on his back.

Quinion knelt by the side of the dog.

'I'll give you two minutes,' he said evenly, 'to disappear. If you don't, I'll thrash you as you've thrashed the dog.'

Kneeling though he was he expected the sudden rush which the other made at him. For a second time the man with the whip somersaulted through the air, landing this time on his face. Moving with great speed for a man of his build, Quinion retrieved the whip and was swishing it through the air as his opponent struggled to his feet. The small eyes seemed to burn.

'I'll murder you. . . .' The voice was thick and the man had difficulty in speaking through lips that were badly bruised where they had hit the earth. 'I'll . . .'

Quinion flicked the whip threateningly, and the other flinched.

'You'll do nothing of the kind,' said Quinion. 'You'll . . . so that's the game.' He broke off suddenly, and closed on the man. There was a flash of steel in the red glow of the setting sun, and a knife dropped from nerveless fingers to the ground. The grip on the man's arm was excruciating; he writhed, completely helpless.

Before Quinion had decided what to do a girl's voice from behind him made him turn round. The girl, or woman, was talking to the dog. Even at that moment Quinion noticed the undeniable quality of her voice.

He released the arm, eyeing the man steadily and pointing towards a hedge which skirted a nearby road.

'You can choose between going now or waiting until I have time to make you wish you were dead. Which is it?'

His tone, and the expression in his eyes, were ice cold. A few people knew that at such a moment Quinion was as dangerous as any man alive. The other man, peering through half-closed eyes, seemed to sense it; he turned on his heel.

'I'll get you,' he said thickly. 'I'll get you for this.'

'Oh, go away,' said Quinion. 'You're objectionable.'

He watched the heavily-built figure moving quickly towards the hedge, and saw the man disappear. 'I wouldn't be surprised to hear from him again,' he reflected.

Turning round, he found himself looking into a pair of hazel eyes which were gazing at him questioningly. The girl was really something. Sun-tanned, clear-skinned, very attractive. She had auburn hair, a green cotton frock, nice legs and ankles.

'Do you live far away?' Quinion inquired. 'Or shall we take him' —the Alsatian whimpered as though acknowledging the thought— 'into Runsey? I know Thomas, the vet.'

'I think it better to get him home,' she said quietly. 'It's not much farther than the village, and I can telephone for Thomas.'

'Right,' said Quinion. 'Then hold his head and forelegs and ease him into my arms . . . slowly . . . that's great.'

He held the Alsatian close to him, and could see the red weals which the whip had made. He wished now that he had thrashed the man with the small eyes.

The girl was talking soothingly to the Alsatian, and Quinion was content to listen to the clear voice, which held a husky hint of Sussex burr. Occasionally he glanced at the profile of his companion. When she returned his glance, she smiled with a frankness which greatly appealed to him.

'We ought to introduce ourselves,' he said. 'My name is Quinn.'

'I'm Margaret Alleyn,' she told him. 'And I can't tell you how grateful I am.'

Quinion, not a particularly impressionable man, felt that there could hardly be a better start than that to an acquaintance.

2

QUINION IS PUZZLED

OAK COTTAGE, the home of Margaret Alleyn, was a picturesque old building of the Tudor period, with shaped oak gables, latticed and shuttered windows and a gnarled, rose-covered porch, combining to create an appearance of delightful old-world stability. The cottage had at one time been the Lodge House of Runsey Hall, before a spend-thrift lord of the manor had made retrenchment necessary—the rooms were furnished in keeping with the great oak rafters and the wide, red-brick fireplaces with their cushioned corner seats.

Quinion was sitting in a comfortable leather arm-chair, smoking a Virginian cigarette and drinking a cup of steaming tea in company with his hostess. He was unusually content; and at odd moments thought almost kindly of the swarthy-faced man whose brutality had made the situation possible—had, in fact, created it.

The more Quinion saw of the girl, the more he liked her. There was a kind of fascination in that near-husky voice and the delicate features. Her hair was darker than he had realized, yet redeemed from sombreness by a sheen which gave it the appearance of fine satin; here and there a gleaming strand of auburn or gold caught the eye, attracting the attention, convincing him more completely than before of its beauty. Her brow, broad, smooth and white, surmounted two gently curling eyebrows, which in turn crowned the large hazel eyes with their silken lashes. In some lights, Jimmy noticed, the hazel of her eyes turned into a glowing molten amber. Her nose, short and straight and a little *retroussé*, led downwards to exquisitely shaped lips whose deep red colouring vied with the flaming roses of June's finest blooms. Her chin was feminine and yet firm, not pointed, not square, but merging perfectly into the features of her beauty. The slender neck sloped downwards to shoulders which Quinion could imagine were creamily white and flawless.

Peter, the Alsatian, was lying on a large rug between his two friends; Thomas, the veterinary surgeon, had been, prescribed treatment, and gone; the dog, he promised them, would be as fit as ever within a few days.

Over the second cigarette the girl broached the subject of the man with the whip. She was smiling, a little nervously, as if she didn't know how to begin. Quinion, who had introduced himself as Mr. James Quinn, was leaning back in his chair.

'It's very difficult to say "thank you", Mr. Quinn, but I am . . . deeply grateful,' she said.

Quinion leaned forward in his chair, waving the cigarette.

'There's no need to say a word. Absolutely none. Anyone would have done exactly the same in similar circumstances—barring gentlemen of the same kidney as our dark-faced friend. The pity is that I turned up too late to be of much help to poor old Peter.'

Margaret Alleyn smiled with her eyes, reflectively, and Quinion had an uneasy feeling that she was laughing at him for some unimaginable reason.

'It isn't a common attribute to be able to throw a man of Loder's weight,' she commented. She paused for a moment, giving Quinion a chance to absorb the shock. So his opponent had been Thomas Loder, the man he was to watch. He tugged a handkerchief from his pocket, disseminating his surprise in a sneeze, and the girl went on: ' . . . as easily as a dog-whip. Is it?'

Quinion's cigarette moved in widening circles.

'It's all a matter of practice,' he assured her. 'Like picking blackberries, simple when you know how.'

'It must be an interesting sight watching you practicing.'

Quinion grinned.

'Touché.' He wanted to approach the matter from a different angle, for he might get to know a great deal about Thomas Loder. 'I take it that the man . . . Loder, did you call him? . . . doesn't make a habit of things like today? Or is it a complex of his?'

The expression clouding the hazel eyes told Quinion better than any words that Thomas Loder was not only known to the girl, but that she felt a dislike which was certainly not characteristic of her. He scented mystery, and was anxious to scent mystery where Thomas Loder was concerned.

'He has been determined to kill Peter,' she told him. 'They've been enemies since Loder first started to visit us here.'

'A friend of the family?' inquired Quinion.

'An acquaintance of my father. I believe that they are working together on some business proposition. My father, you see, is an invalid, and Loder has to call here quite often.'

There was no mistaking the fact that the topic was distasteful, and Quinion had an idea that she had vouchsafed the information solely because she felt she owed him an explanation. It was unfortunate, for Quinion would have liked to have known more about the relationship between the owners of Oak Cottage and the tenant of Cross House. In the circumstances it was impossible to ask more questions without showing too much interest.

'From what I can gather Peter is an excellent judge of character,' he said. 'Loder seems a particularly poisonous personality.'

'He is poisonous . . . and more than that, he's very dangerous. Mr. Quinn'—she leaned forward, her hand touched Quinion's arm— 'is it necessary for you to stay in the neighbourhood?'

There was no doubt of the depth of her feeling. It was all that Quinion could do to cover up his surprise.

'Not absolutely necessary. But surely you're not suggesting that Loder is sufficiently dangerous to make it unpleasant if I keep about here? I mean'—he grinned a little as though in apology— 'I *am* able to look after myself more or less.'

The girl shrugged her shoulders, keeping her eyes averted as she spoke. Quinion assured himself that the mood was not assumed for what she considered the exigency of the moment; Margaret Alleyn was worried. She had been worried for some time; he wondered whether her expression was as much fear as hatred. In any case he would look into it; very decidedly it was a matter which needed investigating.

'I can't explain,' Margaret said. 'I only know that Loder is a man who stops at nothing. He is——'

She broke off and stood up suddenly, looking down with an almost pleading smile into Quinion's face.

'I've already said far more than I should have,' she told him. 'I can only advise you to keep as far away from Loder as you can. If you *have* to meet him again . . . well, he's not unused to firearms.'

She spoke as she looked, scared. Quinion sensed that she really felt she had said too much and would be glad when he was gone. He stood up; this certainly wasn't the time to press for more information.

'I suppose I should be very curious; to be honest, I am. At least let me say this: if you find Loder too objectionable, telephone me at the Tavern in Runsey. I shall be there for the next few days.'

She gave him a smile which held a mixture of appreciation and question. Quinion congratulated himself that her attitude to him was at least perfectly friendly.

'Must you stay there?' she asked.

'I needn't but I mean to.' The purposefulness of which Lady Gloria had caught a glimpse earlier in the afternoon showed clearly. Margaret Alleyn found herself admitting a liking for this clear-eyed, athletic-looking giant of a man. 'I hadn't intended staying longer than over-night—until this afternoon. You see, I've taken rather a fancy to poor old Peter.' He was half laughing. 'For the moment, then . . .'

But his hand was not taken. The colour drained from Margaret's cheeks, and there was no longer any doubt that it was fear which leapt into her eyes.

The Alsatian at their feet growled and glared towards the door, from beyond which had come a sound of men's voices raised in anger. Suddenly there was the ominous report of a revolver shot.

3

DEATH AT OAK COTTAGE

MARGARET ALLEYN had seen the ease with which Quinion had overpowered Loder earlier in the evening, but she was not prepared for the speed at which he jumped for the door, flung it open, and disappeared. She stood waiting to catch any sound from the room into which her visitor had gone. Was this laughing, happy-go-lucky Mr. James Quinn to become mixed up in the strange happenings which had followed her father's association with Thomas Loder?

Quinion had no qualms. In his hand a bluish-grey automatic gleamed, and from his eyes shone determination to discover the source of the revolver shot.

The little room into which he had darted was empty, yet the voices and the shot had definitely come from behind the door. He peered round, taking in the bare furnishings of the room at a glance. It was obviously used as an office. At one end, near a small window, stood a desk littered with papers and the paraphernalia of the usual secretarial sanctum, and a swivel-chair stood in front of it. Two upright chairs, a telephone and two etchings hung from the picture rail separating the distempered ceiling from the psuedo-panelled walls.

But the thing which caught Quinion's eye was the dark, spreading stain on the small piece of carpet beneath the swivel-chair.

It was blood; a moment's inspection satisfied Quinion on that point. But where had the occupants of the room gone? There were no other doors, and the window was too small to permit the exit of a schoolboy; a wounded man could not possibly have been squeezed through. Oak Cottage was living up to the mystery which he had already found to surround Margaret Alleyn.

Obviously there was no point in sounding the wall which separated the office from the room in which Margaret was standing, and it was equally useless to try the wall by the window. Quinion tapped the two which remained, but no hollow echo came. His frown deepened; there must be some way out.

The only remaining possibility was that the floor of the office was movable. It was not a comforting thought, for it offered the chance of being jerked suddenly into a chamber beneath. Quinion was never inclined to take chances which would only end in defeat, and decided that the wise plan was to go back into the room from which he had come. He did not enjoy the idea, for he had a great objection to admitting defeat, especially to the girl, but there was nothing else for it. He opened the door and walked through.

Margaret Alleyn was standing in exactly the same position as when he had left her; only her expression had changed.

Quinion shrugged his shoulders.

'Empty,' he said. 'Was there a shot, or did I dream it?'

He was not prepared for her greeting. Her glance was positively unfriendly, and her chin thrust forward almost accusingly.

'I think,' she told him pointedly, 'that you are outstaying your welcome, Mr. Quinn.' She didn't mean it; she couldn't mean it, no one could change so quickly. Obviously she had suddenly come under some new kind of pressure.

'A matter,' he said quietly, 'which is entirely in your hands, Miss Alleyn. I would like to be welcome to you, but I'm certainly going to be here for a while, welcome or not. Possibly until I can get some information concerning that shot and the injured man which will help the police.'

At the mention of the word 'police' her lips tightened and her fingers clenched the arms of her chair.

'Mr. Quinn, please go.'

It was an appeal which he found hard to resist, but the need for discovering whatever there was to discover about Oak Cottage, and the connection of its owner with Mr. Thomas Loder, made him obstinate. He smiled engagingly without losing the steely purpose obvious in his eyes.

'Let's be frank, Miss Alleyn. This afternoon I ran into the man Loder, and had to move pretty fast to stop him putting a knife in my back. I'm told, by someone who does not appear to be of the type which indulges in flights of fancy, that he is dangerous, and possesses a nasty habit of rushing about with firearms. Shortly afterwards I hear a shot, apparently from a revolver, and find an empty room, although there is no obvious way for anyone to get out of it in so short a time without being seen, and, most important of all, I find a pool of blood. How is it possible for me to leave without trying to discover what has happened? After all, a quarrel can be a private affair, but when it comes to shooting it loses its privacy. Surely you agree.'

Margaret Alleyn closed her eyes with a resignation which made Quinion almost despise himself. She spoke slowly and with considerable effort.

'You are perfectly right. But every minute that you stay here increases the danger to yourself. Mr. Quinn'—her eyes opened, but she was looking towards the window, not at Quinion— 'take my advice. Go, while you can.'

Almost as soon as he saw the sudden alarm of her eyes Quinion was out of his chair and crouching behind it, using the thickly padded back as a shield. He thanked his stars that Margaret had been looking away from him; otherwise he would not have had the warning in time. For a second time that afternoon a revolver shot disturbed the serenity of Oak Cottage, and fast upon it came a third, fired from Quinion's revolver. The glass of the window shattered and from outside came a sharp cry; Quinion had found his target.

Once again Margaret Alleyn was amazed at the speed with which her companion moved. Seizing a stiff-backed chair, he hurled it through the window and leapt onto the sill; for a second time he disappeared from sight as two further shots rang out, followed by a muttered curse and the sound of scuffling.

Quinion scarcely had time to be surprised. He reflected, afterwards, that he had been amazed at finding that his attacker was not Thomas Loder. He was, in fact, an under-sized little man as fair as Loder was dark; but he made up for his lack of inches with a surprising, sinuous strength, and, in spite of the fact that he had been wounded twice by Quinion's sharpshooting, made the big man exert all his strength before he capitulated.

Quinion, sitting astride his assailant's chest, breathed heavily. A ticklish customer, this confrère of Loder's. He eyed the man levelly.

'To what great cause do we owe the honour of this visit?' he demanded, and then added, 'Funny Face.'

Funny Face was certainly no beauty, and a scar running from his forehead to his chin gave him a ferocious expression, helped by a broken nose. He swore.

Quinion shook his head sadly.

'If you ask me,' he reflected, 'you ought to work for someone other than Mr. Loder. That gentleman's vocabulary is anything but edifying. But spill something, or I'll call a policeman.'

Funny Face made a convulsive effort to escape, but thirteen-stone-six of bone and muscle ridiculed the endeavour. Quinion shook his head.

'It's positively time-wasting. You haven't the ghost of a chance of getting up, until you talk. Why not talk?'

Funny Face snarled:

'I'll talk yer, yer bloody smartie. I'll rip yer tongue out.'

Quinion's expression became icy. He held a sneaking admiration for his assailant's obstinacy in the face of defeat, but too much time had been wasted. He pulled his revolver from his pocket, and before Funny Face had realized his intention struck the man heavily on the temple. With a gasping moan, the man collapsed.

Quinion stood up, his lips curved as though he had tasted something unpleasant. He disliked hitting a helpless man but the situation called for haste, there were no handy ropes or cords with which to pinion the fellow, and he meant to take no more chances than were absolutely necessary.

Glancing at the window before preparing to hoist the little man on his shoulder—he intended to take him into the cottage and fasten his hands and legs securely—he altered his plans quickly. Margaret Alleyn was looking at him, and her eyes showed that fear again. Even at that moment Quinion longed to be able to drive that hopelessness away from her, yet he did not neglect the warning. He stepped towards her.

'What is it?' There was no time for preamble, and he spoke curtly.

'There are six or seven of them. . . .' Her voice was so low that he could hardly catch the words, but there was no mistaking the urgent anxiety which she felt. 'For heaven's sake get away if you can. . . .'

'Where are they?' he demanded.

'Coming from Cross Farm. Loder's here. He's telephoning them now. . . .'

'Only Loder?'

'Yes . . . and my father. . . . No! Don't . . .!' Her voice rose as she realized what he meant to do, but he was bent on taking the one chance that he saw of putting Loder out of action for a few days. It was a simple job to climb through the window, and he let himself silently down to the floor. A moment later he regretted his impulse; he found himself gazing into the muzzle of a small, wicked-looking automatic. A gentle voice, coming from a man who sat enveloped in rugs and blankets in an invalid's wheel-chair, greeted him.

'So you have come back.'

Margaret Alleyn turned round quickly, but one thin white hand silenced her as she was about to speak.

'Quiet, my dear. I can handle Mr. Quinn.'

'But, Father——'

The gentle voice resembled nothing more than an icy purr, and the invalid's grey eyes glittered.

'I said "quiet", my dear. You will hear me out, won't you, Mr. Quinn?'

'By all means.' Quinion was smiling, but his mind was working at lightning speed. In the face of that automatic, held amazingly firmly in the sick man's hand, it was risky to

19

try any tricks . . . but Loder might come from the office at any minute, and there was a chance that the invalid's aim might be faulty. 'Always delighted to help in the making of dutiful daughters, Mr. Alleyn . . . you are Mr. Alleyn?'

The invalid inclined his head, and for a second his glittering eyes were averted. That was the moment for which Quinion had been waiting.

Ducking like lightning, he took shelter behind the arm-chair which had already saved him from the effect of one well-directed bullet. By gripping the bottom of it he was able to drag it along towards the door, still keeping the thickness of its padded back between himself and the man with the gun. It was an effective shield, and it enabled him to grip his own automatic. He decided to acquaint Mr. Alleyn of the fact.

'Mr. Alleyn. . . .'

The cold, purring voice responded at once.

'You are not getting cramped, I trust?'

'Oh, not a bit; I'm quite used to this kind of thing; I might almost call myself an expert. No, what I intended to tell you, Mr. Alleyn, is that I have a gun.'

'Indeed.'

'And I can see the wheel of your chair.'

'Is that so?'

'All I want to add,' said Quinion, 'is that I can shoot you, but you can't shoot me. Don't you think your best plan is to throw your gun on the floor?'

'It . . . might . . . be.'

Quinion dropped his tone of casual banter, and his words came harshly. 'I'll give you three seconds to drop it.'

He had scarcely finished before the small automatic dropped to the floor. The invalid obviously believed in discretion. Quinion, however, had played similar games before; he was not fully satisfied.

'Now raise both your hands in the air, Mr. Alleyn—higher—so that I can see them. That's right; keep them there.'

A glance towards the door which led to the office assured him that it was still closed; Loder's telephone talk was a lengthy one. He stood up.

'I think I'll go now . . . I'm not at all sure that I haven't been here too long as it is, Mr. Alleyn. I'll drop in again one day.'

Suddenly his expression hardened. He was looking towards the fireplace, which he had been admiring less than an hour before. His lips were compressed in a thin line, and the glint in his eyes was of rage.

'So that explains it, does it?' He stared into the strangely light-grey eyes of the invalid. 'I have an idea, Mr. Alleyn, that you will find yourself in a very queer fix . . . when you have to tell twelve good men and true just why there is a dead man propped up in your fireplace.'

Almost as he spoke the body, which was fixed stiffly into the corner of the cushioned seat, began to move. It sent a chilling horror to his spine as he stared at the hole gaping in the forehead of the dead man, which was the more gruesome as the body toppled slowly towards the ground, falling on to the floor with a sickening crash.

4

A Man Named Smith

THE Hon. James Quinion had been in many tight corners, from all of which he had extricated himself by the
exercise of that ingenuity which made him a valued agent of
the Department called 'Z' at Whitehall. Moreover, he possessed a dogged tenacity in the face of difficulty and a flair
for probing intricate problems with a keenness which rarely
lost its edge. He was, in fact, extremely resourceful.

The situation at Oak Cottage, however, presented him
with a problem which possessed many factors that might
easily lead to his downfall. Outside was the little man with
the scar, unconscious when Jimmy had left him, but liable
to wake up at any time and to prove himself ravenous for
vengeance; and he had a revolver. In the office, according
to Margaret Alleyn, Thomas Loder was telephoning to Cross
Farm; he was taking a long time to deliver his message, but
he might be expected to open the door at any moment.
In all probability, he too possessed a revolver. And coming
from Cross Farm, if the girl's information was true, were
seven men, summoned by Loder and presumably imbued
with that swarthy gentleman's unpleasant habits.

Quinion ran through the possibility of escape. He might try the window, but it meant turning his back on the invalid, Alleyn, or the probably recovering Funny Face. He might try the door, but it meant taking the chance of running into a small contingent of Loder's faithful seven. Finally, he might force his way past Alleyn to the third door of the room, which undoubtedly led to the back of the cottage, but it meant chancing the appearance of Funny Face at the window, Loder at the door of the office, and another likely contingent of the attacking seven. His only ally, and a fickle one at that, was luck.

He decided to act normally and to go out by the door, for his back was almost touching it and he could get out more quickly. His hand was on the handle when he heard the sound of a car engine approaching the cottage. Either the seven had arrived, or yet another complication had cropped up; in any case, it barred the front door as a means of exit. He looked across at Alleyn; the invalid's light-grey eyes were fixed on his with an expression of cold malevolence. The silky voice purred.

'It isn't going to be quite so simple as you had hoped, is it?'

'Maybe you're right,' Quinion admitted. 'On the other hand, it might be a small army belonging to the local constabulary.'

A flash of doubt sprang into the invalid's eyes. Whatever else, Quinion had no doubt as to the dread in which the Alleyns, both father and daughter, held all thought of the police. The mystery of Oak Cottage was both deep and ugly, and the 'business proposition' being discussed between Alleyn and Loder was definitely outside the law.

'What makes you think it might be the police?' demanded Alleyn. 'You are not a policeman?'

Quinion chuckled.

'Not yet, but you never know. After this little do the lads at Scotland Yard might hanker after my services; on the other hand, they might not. No, Alleyn. I am not a policeman. But five loud revolver shots have hit the air recently, and you're not far from the main road, are you?'

The invalid's momentary tension eased.

'You are hoping for the best, eh, Mr. Quinn? An admirable trait, but in this instance unlikely to be vindicated. I wonder how long Loder is likely to be at that telephone?'

'To tell you the truth,' confessed Jimmy, 'I'd rather like to know that myself. Meanwhile . . .' He moved away from the door quickly as he heard footsteps outside and felt the woodwork quiver as someone pushed against it. A second later came three short raps. From the sudden concentration in Alleyn's eyes, and the involuntary gasp which fell from Margaret's lips—it was the first sound she had made since Quinion had climbed through the window and her father had spoken to her—Quinion knew that it was unexpected.

Not one of the three spoke, however, and the caller rapped again, impatiently.

It was time, Quinion decided, that he took some action, and he acted quickly. Gathering the arm-chair in his arms he carried it to the door which led to the office; he had noticed that it opened towards the living room; and by pushing the heavy chair against it, was able to guard against a surprise attack from Loder. Then he took his stand near the girl, first picking up the automatic which Alleyn had dropped, and standing so that the body of the dead man was hidden from sight of anyone entering at the door.

'Now,' he said softly, 'you can ask your visitor in, Mr. Alleyn.' He smiled meaningly. 'Only don't forget that my gun is in my pocket—and my hand is holding the gun.'

The invalid nodded. Quinion, his mind filled with a medley of thoughts, could not fail to see the tremendous personality of the sick man, making up in strength of mind, Quinion imagined, what he lacked in strength of limb.

Alleyn raised his voice.

'Come in,' he called. 'You will find the door open.'

The handle turned. The girl, her nerves obviously at breaking point, shuddered a little, and Quinion grinned at her with a confidence that he did not feel. The adventure with the dog had led to a nightmarish situation which had long since been beyond his control. As near as his philosophy permitted, he prayed for luck.

He could not tell immediately whether his prayers had been answered, for the caller was a complete stranger. A tall man and thin, he was dressed in a blue lounge suit of perfect cut, toney brown shoes and trilby hat which he carried in his hand. His face was unremarkable, but a pair of blue eyes redeemed it from actual plainness. He possessed a jaw, too, which suggested considerable strength of character.

A moment's hesitation, whilst he looked quickly at each one of the three, preceded his first words.

'Mr. Arnold Alleyn?'

His eyes were fixed on Quinion, but that worthy motioned silently to the invalid. Alleyn was surveying the newcomer, his body hunched a little, his light-grey eyes bird-like, and his long, tapering fingers intertwining.

'Yes. My name is Alleyn.'

The caller nodded and Quinion began to believe more strongly than ever in his luck; there was a definite antagonism in the visitor's expression. Something akin to puzzlement crept into those fine blue eyes too.

It was not unnatural, for the attitude of the three people in the room was strained. The girl, in spite of her efforts, could not hide her tension; the invalid, although completely self-possessed, created the impression that he was listening for an expected sound, or else awaiting developments along a definite line. And Quinion was trying to watch all three—including the newcomer—whilst keeping an eye on the window for the possible reappearance of Funny Face.

'Thank you.' The caller was obviously nonplussed by the presence of the younger man and the girl. He seemed to deliberate as to whether it was wise to ask for an interview with Alleyn alone, but decided to introduce himself first. 'My name is Smith, Mr. Alleyn. . . .'

Before Quinion had time to observe the reaction of the invalid to this unembarrassing confession, the chair which was propped against the door of the office moved. The door shook and opened a fraction of an inch, without yielding enough for anyone to see inside the room. The voice of Thomas Loder rasped out:

'What the devil is the matter, Alleyn? Who's holding the door?'

Quinion's hand stretched out swiftly and closed over the invalid's mouth. In a soft, silky voice which might have been Alleyn's own, he answered quickly:

'Just a minute, Loder. A chair's slipped under the handle. I'm coming. . . .'

'Then hurry. But be careful of Quinn. Is he in there?'

Quinion's voice aped the invalid's again.

'No. I think he's outside the window . . . wounded in the leg, Loder. I won't be long.'

Quinion had moved now to the side of Mr. Smith. The latter's expression was remarkably cool; it was almost, Quinion thought, as if he had been prepared for a strange reception.

The element of surprise, however, if it missed Mr. Smith, was not long absent from the room. For Quinion was startled out of his self-possession by the sudden appearance of a revolver in Smith's lean brown hand. Quinion's own fingers gripped the automatic in his pocket comfortingly.

'Just what part,' demanded Mr. Smith in an undertone, 'do you hold in the schemes of Alleyn and Loder?'

Quinion arched his brows. He was still standing in the stranger's line of vision, so that the body of the dead man was out of sight.

'None, Mr. Smith, none at all, beyond the misfortune of having butted in on what appears to be a home for inebriates. I was lucky, though; I had a revolver, and it's still in my pocket . . . and in my hand.'

His own flecked grey eyes were less than a yard from the clear blue ones of the newcomer. They contemplated each other for a moment, before Mr. Smith smiled slightly.

'I'll take your word for it,' he assured Quinion. His revolver veered round, pointing towards the door of the office, from whence proclamations of Loder's growing impatience were plainly audible. 'Don't you think you could let Loder out? He likes surprises.'

Quinion nodded. He moved towards the door but a gasp from Margaret Alleyn stopped him and he looked quickly towards the window in time to see the eyes and broken nose of Funny Face above the window sill. He darted back towards the front door, speaking rapidly to the man called Smith.

'Take my tip,' he said urgently, 'and get out of here while the going's good. We're outnumbered five to one.'

As though in support of his words the sound of heavy footsteps and muttering voices came from the office. Above them Loder's thick tones raised in command.

'Crash down that door. I don't like the way things are going.'

The arm-chair shivered as the door was subjected to the impact of several hefty shoulders. Mr. Smith, to Quinion's relief, had no hankering after mock heroics; he had opened the front door and was waiting on the threshold, his revolver held ready for emergency.

'Start your engine,' Quinion said quickly, 'and keep an eye open for the man who was at the window . . . although I fancy he's gone round to the back entrance. I'll be with you in a moment.'

He looked at the girl as Smith hurried towards his car. The oak door of the office was already bulging, and Loder's voice was still raised in profane exhortation.

'Are you staying here?' Quinion asked.

The girl nodded briefly. Her body was still held taut, but there was an aloofness in her eyes which puzzled Quinion. What part in the plans of Loder and her father did Margaret Alleyn play?

Alleyn's silky voice answered him.

'Of course, Mr. Quinn. What else could a dutiful daughter do?'

Quinion waited for nothing more. Already the panels of the oak door were splitting under the onslaught of half a dozen men.

'Don't forget,' he called out over his shoulder, 'that telephone call. . . .' He was out of sight now, racing towards the small car—a Singer—at the wheel of which the man called Smith was sitting in readiness. He leapt into it. The car moved off, accelerated far more roughly than its makers intended. The two men were fifty yards along the lane which led to the main road before Quinion, looking back, saw five or six men running towards the car, and heard a dozen ineffectual revolver shots.

He grinned, remembering Loder's vocabulary after he had been thwarted from his desire to kill the Alsatian.

'Ten to one Mr. Blooming Loder will want a new dictionary. He would be worth hearing at the moment.'

The man called Smith darted a look at his companion. His lips were set in a thin, hard line.

'The only thing that Loder is worth,' he said grimly, 'is killing and killing painfully.'

But Quinion barely heard him. He was thinking of a pair of deep hazel eyes which had so suddenly become afraid.

5

DEPARTMENT 'Z'

THE Hon. James Quinion, *alias* Mr. Quinn, sat in the private parlour of the Tavern, Runsey, alternately discussing strange happenings with a man named Smith and quaffing a foamy beverage looking like and tasting like the stuff called beer. An hour had passed since the two men had escaped from Oak Cottage and its murderous inhabitants, and in that time Quinion had learned many things.

He had first given Smith the full story of his adventures of the evening, leaving out nothing but the arrival of the telegram from Department 'Z', which meant, of course, that he had not informed his companion that he had had suspicions of Thomas Loder even before that worthy's ferocious attack on the dog. He had explained his possession of a revolver by saying that shooting was a hobby; which was not strictly true, for shooting was very nearly his most serious business in life. The man named Smith had not been aware of the reticence, however, and had responded admirably to Jimmy's confidences.

Smith said that he was a Canadian by birth, and it was on the occasion of one of his frequent trips to his native country that he had first met Thomas Loder. Smith was the owner of an extensive ranch in Manitoba, through which ran a small river; the river, of course, being the cause of the fruitfulness of his ranch—wheat mainly, with some cattle and orchard land. Loder had purchased a smaller farm adjacent to Smith's, and in the latter's absence had bribed the manager of the big farm to let his cattle graze on pasture land already too small for Smith's own cattle. There had been a bitter struggle, a lawsuit and the complete rout of Thomas Loder. Which, in the opinion of the man named Smith, was just as it should have been. He held a very different opinion about the habit which Loder developed of rustling his cattle and driving herds through vast stretches of wheat land, completely ruining the crops.

It did not last long, of course; Loder found the country too hot to hold him, but not until he had played such havoc with Smith's farm that the latter was forced to sell out. In consequence the Canadian began a bitter search for his enemy, who had left Canada officially for England.

Smith confessed to wanting nothing more than to achieve the complete ruination of Thomas Loder, and for several years had held on the trail, learning more and more of Loder's habits. After a while he became convinced that the activities of the other were criminal; by chance he stumbled on to the fact that Loder had a connection of some kind with practically every town in England, always with its doubtful elements. The man named Smith decided to inform the police; on several occasions he had been nearer sudden death than he relished.

It was here that Quinion began to sit up; the police, said Smith, received him blandly, promised to investigate, and yet did nothing at all, in spite of the fact that they had been given ample evidence to convict Loder of a dozen crimes which would have put the man behind bars for seven years at least. After three interviews at Scotland Yard, Smith had decided that his only course was to keep on Loder's trail himself, and in the course of his efforts had discovered the connection between Mr. Arnold Alleyn and the man upon whom the police looked with such benevolent eyes. Quinion knew the result of Smith's one and only interview with Alleyn.

Quinion, having listened with flattering interest to his companion's story, suddenly awakened to the fact that his beer had run out. The man named Smith did not conceal his irritation at Quinion's seeming opinion that beer was more important than the story of a feud which had lasted several years, but Jimmy proceeded to allay suspicions of his sanity.

'The fact is,' he said confidingly, 'I'm not used to stunts like this afternoon's affair. I need a stimulant. But what I want to know, Smith, is the nature of Loder's criminal habits. Does he wander about robbing people, or killing them, or does he go in for politics?'

The man called Smith grinned in spite of himself.

'I'd be very interested myself,' he answered finally. 'For two years he travelled England thoroughly, and found a welcome with a certain type of lawyer and men whom the local police knew as fences. I know for a fact that he has bought and sold jewellery although fully aware that it was stolen—it was on this account that I went to Scotland Yard—but I've an idea that jewels are only a side-line.'

'Why?' interjected Quinion, from the mouth of a tankard.

The Canadian shrugged his shoulders.

'I couldn't have said as much six months ago, but since Loder rented Cross Farm he has made three trips to the continent—one to France, one to Western Germany and one to Moscow—and each time he has been received by influential members of the extremist parties . . . in Moscow he was greeted like a compatriot.'

Quinion nearly choked himself in a sudden anxiety to speak.

'Politics!' he spluttered finally, 'politics! There you are, Smith, I told you so. . . .'

Once again the Canadian appeared to think that his companion was not treating the matter as seriously as he should do, and once again Quinion consoled him.

'It's like this,' he said quietly. 'In Runsey I have a reputation as a—well, they call me Archie. That charming damsel . . . the barmaid; she can't be more than fifty-five, Smithy . . . is probably straining her ears to catch the lastest gem of wit from my ruby lips, and later in the evening Loder, or one of his henchmen, will probably look in and talk to the angel. "What," he will ask, "did they talk about?" "Oh," she will simper, "Archie was *just* as *mad* as *ever*! Ain't he a *scream*?" Which is another way of saying that Loder or the Loderite will get little in the way of change. So if you think I'm just a little queer . . . put it down to that.'

Smith eyed his companion with a new respect. Quinion *did* not let him reflect too deeply, however.

'All of which,' Quinion said lightly, 'might be all my-eye-and-Betty-Martin; but on the other hand it might not. As a personal opinion, Smith, I always prefer a two-barrel gun if I haven't an automatic, which is another way of saying that if one don't hit, the other might not miss. Follow me?'

Smith nodded.

'It's right with me,' he commented, filling his pipe—the private parlour was thick with the smoke from two overworked briars—and eyeing Quinion steadily with his calm blue eyes.

'You seem to have hit on Loder by chance, but it strikes me that what you've seen hasn't scared you; I mean, you aren't scared of guns and things.'

'I revel in 'em,' confessed Quinion. 'Life for me should be one scrap after another . . . or just one all the time; one all the time, I think; it would be more settling.'

Smith smiled.

'That's just it. Now, Loder is too big a handful for me alone . . . why not join up?' He looked almost anxious; the task of running Mr. Thomas Loder to earth had developed along much more dangerous lines than he had anticipated, and the strain was beginning to tell.

Quinion sought courage from his tankard before answering. His expression was light-hearted and his lips were curled in a humorous line.

'Strictly between ourselves,' he said, 'I've a hankering to see Loder in a coffin or in a cell; his methods don't attract me, and that poor devil who was killed this afternoon needs a little avenging . . . forgive me if that's melodrama. In the last few hours I've developed an interest which might be called feminine . . . I'll explain why I say that in a minute. If I could keep in the neighbourhood for a while, I would, like a shot; but I must go up to town to-night, and my visit might last two or three days; it's out of my hands.

'I can manage this, however. Several of my friends in London have a yearning after the gay life and use-your-pistols, and I'll have a chat with one or two of them in the morning. If I can't get back myself, I'll send them along; meanwhile, I'd like to feel that someone was close handy in case Miss Alleyn feels like telephoning to the Tavern; I told her to if things get too warm. Have I made sense?'

The Canadian nodded.

'Yes. Although I'll be surprised if Loder hasn't enough for one day.'

'That's the way I look at it,' admitted Quinion. 'Anyhow, I'm hoping that I shall be able to get back here before any more trouble starts. However, if I don't, and if anyone pops along and says that Archie sent them, you'll know who they are.'

'Surest thing,' affirmed Smith.

'Splendid!' Quinion emptied his tankard and stood up, eyeing his companion steadily.

'Listen,' he said slowly. 'If anything happens . . . and no one turns up . . . put a trunk call through to London and ask for "Victoria Nought". Tell whoever answers you . . . and don't ask who it is, because they'll ring off; make quite sure of that . . . just as much as you can; if you need help, you'll get it.' He extended his hand suddenly. 'Don't forget that one about the girl and the . . .' He broke off into a cackle of laughter, his shoulders quaking as he walked to the door. The Canadian's last vision of him was a hand chucking the chin of a grinning barmaid.

Three hours later, at a time when all true members of the fraternity of rich young men, of which Quinion was a prominent example, were making a final choice between the blonde at the extreme right of the chorus and the brunette in the middle; the blonde, being a trifle plumper, was getting most votes—Quinion was climbing out of a Bristol in front of a house which lay in one of the streets leading from Whitehall. He was in evening dress, and the scent of his pomade vied with the perfume of his Egyptian cigarette for the first place in horrors. A less fortunate citizen, had he seen Quinion disappearing into the doorway of the house, would have said darkly: 'One o' them there gamin' plices, I betcher a dollar.' In a measure it would have been true; the chief of Department 'Z' of the War Office gambled in the lives of men and of nations.

The Hon. James Quinion had no illusions; whatever mission he was sent on might easily end in death. But at the moment his chief concern was of the Egyptian cigarette, for he was convinced that if he smoked another half an inch of it he would expire.

6

MR. GORDON CRAIGIE

NO ONE who entered the sparsely furnished room in which Gordon Craigie spent eighteen hours out of most twenty-four worried much about the apartment or its appointments. Craigie was perhaps the least known man in England; he might be concerned in a motor accident, but his name never appeared; he might give an opinion which would change the whole trend of diplomatic relations between one great Power and another, but his name never appeared. At the secret conclaves of the Inner Cabinet he was spoken of as 'Z'; it was a remarkable fact that one popular and successful Prime Minister reigned for four years and was in continual contact with Department 'Z' without setting eyes on nor learning the name of the man who was known by reputation alone in every country in the world.

Craigie was less a personality than a presence, creating an atmosphere as he sat, immobile, in a swivel-chair in front of a polished desk which at no time held more than one file of papers; at least, no one but Craigie himself had ever seen two files on it. At his elbow was a telephone, and at his side a dictaphone, the cylinders of which were typed in the room and destroyed in front of his own eyes.

The room itself was unremarkable, being furnished very much after the manner of most offices, but possessing a brown leather arm-chair, a gas ring and a cabinet containing the necessities for minor creature comforts, next to the fireplace; the small area about which looked very much like any ordinary bachelor's hearth, although usually shielded by a large screen from the eyes of Gordon Craigie's many visitors.

One thing with which every visitor was cognizant was that the walls of the room were steel-lined, that its one window was fitted with unbreakable glass, and its one door could not open without Craigie pressing a button.

It was into this room that the Hon. James Quinion, *alias* Mr. Quinn, walked calmly on the night of his adventures with Thomas Loder. Quinion had first met Gordon Craigie when the latter had given up all thought of ever seeing a human face again . . . that was ten years before, when Craigie had taken a more active part, physically, in the work of the Department, and Quinion, an exuberant youth of twenty-three, had stumbled by accident on a network of intrigue which had delighted his excitement-loving soul. In consequence the relationship between the two men was of firm friendship, cemented on Quinion's side by a respect which was almost reverence; not that his attitude of light-hearted *camaraderie* reflected that reverence.

Quinion threw two inches of Egyptian cigarette into the empty fire-grate, heaved a sigh of relief, smiled at the older man, who was sitting in the arm-chair in front of the hearth. Slinging off his light coat, his hat and his gloves, he dragged the swivel-chair from the desk and sat down opposite his chief.

'I've come,' he announced.

Craigie slung a well-filled tobacco pouch, from which Quinion proceeded to cram his pipe. The chief of Department 'Z' was regarding his companion contemplatively, his keen grey eyes unwinking, his hooked nose twitching a little at the nostrils. A meerschaum drooped on to his chest, creating an incongruous impression that he was taking life easily; it was incongruous because those piercing grey eyes were ever alert, and the man's whole body, even in repose, suggested tremendous energy, both mental and physical.

'If you ask me,' commented Quinion, slinging the pouch back, 'you ought to have been a Red Indian, Gordon . . . or a witch doctor; you look just like one.'

Craigie's lips twitched a little at the corners; it was the nearest approach that he ever achieved to a smile. Quinion's comparison, however, was not inept, for his chief possessed just that impassive alertness for which the North American natives are renowned; and the drooping meerschaum added to the similarity. Moreover, Craigie was notoriously a man of few words.

'What happened at Runsey?' he demanded.

Quinion settled himself more comfortably, placing his feet on the low mantel-shelf.

'Many things, old man—many nasty and unpleasant things. As a matter of fact, I'm not a bit sure that I haven't mucked the whole show, as far as I'm concerned. It got out of hand.'

'Start from the beginning,' said Craigie.

Quinion plunged immediately into a narration of the events which had followed so quickly upon each other after he had received the telegram from Department 'Z', and had started on his surveyance of Cross Farm. Gordon

Craigie listened without a comment, his only movements being to take the drooping pipe from his mouth at regular intervals.

'So you see,' said Quinion, 'I haven't looked at Cross Farm yet, and I've made Loder keep his eye open for me.'

'Under the name of Quinn?' The question was rapped out.

'Yes. James Quinn.'

'Go on,' invited Craigie, shifting his position a little.

'Which is another way of saying,' continued Quinion, 'that I forgot, in effect, that I was Number 7 of Department "Z".' He was under no illusions as to the manner of his activities, knowing full well that, having failed to act strictly according to his instructions, he had invited expulsion from the organization of the Department; that he had been unable to help himself mattered not at all; actually there had been no need to butt in on the incident of the dog; and Department 'Z' did not allow for side-lines, even of a humanitarian nature. 'That's not quite all, Gordon.'

For the first time Quinion stirred under the steady gaze of those piercing grey eyes. He knew that one of the strictest rules of Department 'Z' was that no personal element was allowed to interfere with the activities of its members, and he was disturbed in his mind about the effect of a pair of glowing, hazel eyes, a face that was quite beautiful, and a figure that was quite remarkable.

Had Gordon Craigie been less of a friend he might have pushed the subject to the back of his mind without prejudicing his position as an agent of the most skilled organization in the world.

He stood up suddenly, his jaw set, his flecked grey eyes matching Craigie's with a suggestion of dogged determination.

'It's like this. On previous stunts I've been concerned with nothing but the Department's side of the question. I had no scruples about using everything and everybody, providing I could get to the bottom of the trouble. This time . . .'

Gordon Craigie's lips were twitching and the piercing eyes softened strangely. No man but a keen student of nature could have held the reins of Department 'Z'.

'The girl, eh? Knocked you cold.'

Quinion banged one fist into the other open palm.

'Gordon, I want to get her out of the mess. I don't give a damn whether she's in it up to the neck. . . . I want to handle it so that she doesn't pay, if there's anything she should pay for.' He stopped, and lowered himself into the swivel-chair. When he went on his voice was steadier, yet equally emphatic. 'What's more, I'm going to; which is another way of offering my resignation. . . .' He laughed, a little uneasily. 'Nice kind of mess to fall into, isn't it? I'm sorry, Gordon. . . .'

Gordon Craigie held his meerschaum between his fingers, eyeing his friend calmly. He made one of the longest speeches which Quinion had ever heard from him.

'It isn't as bad as all that, Jimmy; there's no need to talk about resigning yet. As a matter of fact, if Loder thinks your interest in him is because of the girl, it'll do more good than harm; he won't know that we're after him. You can stay down there as Mr. James Quinn . . . the villagers don't know you as the Hon. James Quinion, do they?

'James Quinn is officially a cousin of Quinion,' answered the younger man. 'I've found it useful to have a double.'

'Then that's all right. Now listen to me. If I thought there was any danger of you slacking off Loder because of the girl, I'd say "quit", and someone else could take

your place; but I have a feeling that it'll make you keener.
So forget that part of it. For the rest . . . this man named
Smith. I've heard about him from the police. His story
is true, word for word, and he's likely to be very useful
indeed; let him work with you, but don't enlarge on
"Victoria Nought"; he'll be quite satisfied without learning any more about it.

'Meanwhile I can tell you this. Loder is someone near
the top of one of the biggest schemes we've ever come up
against. I don't know much about it yet, but I'm getting
information through almost hourly. I thought at one time
that it was one of the "world for the people" campaigns,
but I'm not sure that it isn't deeper than that. It will come
to nothing, of course, but it might get devilish dangerous
and stir up far more mud than we want, so it'll have to be
strangled as quickly as possible.

'I've an idea that Loder is calling a meeting at Cross
Farm within the next week or two, and that's the reason that
I want the farm watched. I hadn't catered for his having a
small army of gunmen, though. . . .'

Gordon Craigie broke off to fill his pipe, and Quinion
eyed his steady movements with a feeling akin to veneration.
The younger man smiled suddenly as his companion blew a
cloud of grey smoke from the charred meerschaum; White
Chief Craigie. . . .

Craigie went on slowly. His new-found spate of words
seemed to be drying up.

'Once or twice in other affairs you've co-opted a few
temporary members——'

'Yes,' nodded Quinion.

'I think that they might be useful again,' said Craigie.
'Haul them in, and pitch them the story of the damsel in
distress.'

Quinion heaved himself out of the chair, and reached for his coat.

'I'll drop on 'em now. There's just one other thing. . . .'

'What?' demanded the chief, his lips twitching.

'If you were human, and dabbled in beer, I'd drink your health; as you aren't human—thanks. . . .'

'Get out,' said Gordon Craigie; and he actually smiled.

7

THE CAFÉ OF CLOUDS

A SLOW, sleepy melody crept through the large, dim-lighted chamber, lending a magic to the hour and making men forget all but the delights and dreams of illusion. Small tables, shaped like clouds and painted white and grey, with an occasional hint of black, were placed round the sides, next to the walls which, like the scenery of a stage, were made to look as the cool sky of a summer eve above the smiling blue waters of a calm sea. Electric lamps, their glow diffused through shades which merged into the billowing white and grey of the ceiling lent mystery; emptied of men and women, the chamber might have been a very corner of the sky.

The Café of Clouds, however, was not designed to be empty of men and women. The black and white of dinner jackets threw into splendid relief the colours of the women's dresses. Every table was full, every chair occupied, every tails-clad waiter moving with ease about the host of pleasure-seekers, whose latest whim gave popularity to the new-found haunt. Wine flowed. Wine of countless vineyards, from the Rhine and the Loire, from Italy and Spain. On a dais at the

end of the room a band played, against its background of
sky, with every instrument merged into the serene colouring
of the scene; and its melodies were haunting, crooning a
reversion from beat and pop.

In the middle of the room a parquet floor, shimmering and reflecting the clouds of the ceiling, held a dozen
couples, waltzing slowly to that flowing rhythm.

It was strange in such a place that two vacant-looking
young men should be seated at a table by themselves; the
Café of Clouds was not a club at which young men were
wont to sup unaccompanied. From their appearance they
were bored, realizing their loneliness and vainly striving to
console themselves with brandy.

The door, flecked like the walls, opened suddenly, and
a waiter entered, carrying a chair; immediately behind him
came a tall, clear-eyed young man with crisp, dark hair shin-
ing with oil. He was dressed immaculately, and he looked
completely at home. Following the waiter, he was delayed
for a moment at several tables, exchanging a word with one
dazzling creature after another and ignoring many an invita-
tion to join a small party. Obviously he was a popular young
man and well known; a dozen eyes were turned towards him
as he sat in the chair with the two lonely males, who had
made room at their table for the newcomer.

'Jimmy,' said the more vacant-looking young man, 'you
ought to be shot.'

Quinion offered him an Egyptian cigarette, which was
refused with a gesture of abhorrence.

'All right,' he said calmly, putting his case away. 'Then
I'll have one of yours.'

The sad young man found a gold case in his pocket,
opened it and offered it. The monogram informed anyone who cared to examine it closely that the initials were

'R.C.'; his name, known to practically every occupant of the café, was Reginald Chane. His companion, whose first sign of animation for ten minutes accompanied his acceptance of a cigarette, was equally well known as Peter de Lorne. All three young men were prominent members of a society called 'The New Squares'. Peter de Lorne had obviously been thinking of Chane's greeting, and as obviously shared the sentiment, but was finding some difficulty in supporting it without repetition. After several minutes he gave up.

'Yes,' he murmured. 'You ought to be shot.'

'Pleasure,' acknowledged the Hon. James, showing no inclination to resent the attack. He sipped the brandy thoughtfully, gazing about the Café of Clouds. 'Nice little company, he said finally. 'Who's the new blonde with the overdeveloped front?'

Peter de Lorne closed his eyes and Reginald Chane screwed his lips in an expression of sheer disdain.

'She isn't new,' de Lorne vouchsafed finally. 'She's a hag. She was here on Monday, and to-night's Wednesday; the really latest is the auburn-haired wench near the guitar; she's the latest from New York, but I'm damned if I think she's worth a second look. Do you?'

Quinion, gazing lazily across the room, examined the powdered neck and shoulders of the latest from New York. Her face was turned away from him, and he could only see a suggestion of a profile.

'Scraggy,' he said definitely. 'The Aryan race is running out, Peter. Not that it matters much.'

There was a hint of expectancy in the eyes of his two companions, and he grinned amiably.

'I have been hunting,' he announced. 'A real, live man-hunt of a breed which is *not* running out; oh, quite definitely not running out; in fact, there's half a dozen of them all ready to put up a nice little fracas if anyone cares to have a go at them.'

'Tell us more,' implored Mr. de Lorne, looking more than ever incapable of action.

For twenty minutes Quinion talked and smoked. At least five young and hopeful women who were dissatisfied with their escorts at the Café of Clouds were convinced that the eligible Jimmy was discussing them, and less experienced young men than the three who sat in such an austere state of bachelordom would have wilted under the thousand glances from limpid eyes. None of them appeared to be affected, however.

'So now you have it,' Quinion said at last. 'You know just as much as I do.'

'Don't lie,' interjected Reginald Chane listlessly. 'You're a dark horse, Jimmy.'

Quinion patted his friend's hand soothingly.

'Don't you worry, Reginald. You know just as much as is good for you, if not more. The thing is, will you be up early enough in the morning to get to Runsey moderately early?'

'About twelve?' suggested de Lorne hopefully.

'About twelve my grandmother. The Loder lout will have had time to kill half England by then. Nine o'clock.'

De Lorne groaned and Reginald Chane grimaced.

'He's at it again,' grumbled the latter, eyeing the Hon. James with disfavour. 'The last time, you kept us up all night.'

'Right you are,' said Quinion, looking round for a waiter. 'I'll pop along and see what one or two of the other boys think about it.'

'Listen,' interrupted Chane, laying a detaining hand on his arm. 'Just what do you want us to do to Loder if we see him? Sandbag him? Or pepper the blighter with a blunderbuss?'

'All I want you to do is go to the Tavern at Runsey, ask for the man named Smith . . . blue eyes, a jaw, six-feet-one-and-a-bit but skinny . . . and tell him that Archie sent you. Tell him, too, that I'll be down later in the day. Then wait for something to happen . . . and if you've half a chance, get Margaret Alleyn clear of that cottage.'

'Kidnap her?' inquired de Lorne, with sudden interest.

'Harm a hair of her head and your life won't be worth four-and-sixpence, Peter; nor yours, Reginald.' He took another glance round the crowded room, sparing a second for the latest thing from New York.

The brunette's face was turned towards him, and for a moment Quinion felt as though the ground had been taken from under his feet. De Lorne, whose air of listlessness covered a catlike power of observation, saw his friend's fingers tighten suddenly about the slim stem of his wineglass; a second later the stem snapped in two, while Quinion was grinning foolishly at the broken glass.

'What's biting?' demanded de Lorne.

Quinion was displaying his most asinine grin, but the expression in his flecked grey eyes was steely. He glanced round again, however, towards the girl, smiling inanely at an acquaintance at the next table. For the first time he saw the girl's companion, and he ran a thick forefinger round the edge of his collar as though suddenly feeling the heat of the room.

'You needn't go to Runsey,' he said briefly. 'The "latest thing" is Miss Margaret Alleyn, and her companion . . .'

De Lorne looked across at the swarthy-faced man who had been hidden previously by a couple who had got up to dance. He was a thick-set fellow, with small, piglike eyes.

'Loder?' he suggested.

'Loder,' affirmed Quinion, holding out his hand for a cigarette. 'Now, what the devil are they doing here together?

And who told you that she came from New York? . . .' He broke off irritably at a weak chuckle from Reginald Chane; Reginald looked for all the world as though he had just heard the choicest joke ever.

'What is getting you, Pie Face?' he demanded.

Chane endeavoured to triumph over his urgent desire for laughter, but it was not a complete triumph, for his words were interspersed with giggling laughs, making Quinion ache to hit him. De Lorne's brows were cocked inquiringly.

'He—he called—he called her . . .' the exhausted Reginald's chin nearly touched the table as he doubled up. ' . . . oh, boy! He called her *scraggy*! . . .' He leaned back in his chair weakly, just saved from prostration. 'But don't you dare harm a hair of her head, Peter. . . .'

For a moment Quinion struggled between indignation and amusement. His sense of humour gained the day finally, and he grinned, but without enthusiasm.

'I suppose it is funny,' he conceded. 'But mind that wineglass, Reggy, or it'll cost us more in damages than in drinks.' He drummed the table with his fingers. 'Who in this wide, wide world would have thought it? And how are we going to discover what it means?'

De Lorne smoothed his cheek with pale, manicured fingers.

'Sure you haven't hit a miss, Jimmy? Did the girl put one over you?'

Quinion who had acted on Gordon Craigie's advice, and pictured the girl as being under the thumb of her father when relating the story to de Lorne and Chane—shook his head slowly.

'I don't think so. I tell you that she's only doing what she's forced to do. The best thing to do is to carry on as we'd arranged. You two get off, sleep for a few hours, and then go down to Runsey. Loder and the girl may be returning by car to-night. I'll stay here and keep an eye on them. If they've a London rendezvous, I'll find where it is. All right?'

'Right with me,' responded Chane, who had recovered from his near-hysteria sufficiently to cast admiring glances at a scantily dressed damosel for whose dance the floor had been cleared—she was being far more South Sea Island-ish than the most confirmed South Sea Islander—and who displayed some reluctance in going, despite his words. 'Of course, you would say "shoot" just when the star turn of the evening rolls up, wouldn't you, curse you?'

'Stop indulging your baser instincts,' commented de Lorne, craning his neck to get a better view of the dancer. 'She's got a nice turn of speed.'

'Very nice,' agreed Chane. 'There's only one thing the matter with her, Peter.'

'Being?' demanded de Lorne suspiciously.

'Scraggy!' answered Reginald, with a prodigious wink.

Quinion had been too pre-occupied with his thoughts to notice the gibe, however, and his wave of the hand as the two young men left the table was equally absent-minded. Margaret Alleyn and this girl from New York—New York was the then Big Noise in musical comedy—seemed to occupy two separate and distinct personalities; anyone less like an actress of the undress age than the girl of Oak Cottage he found hard to imagine; but it was her all right; her features had become etched on his mind too deeply to allow for the possibility of a mistake. He settled down to wait until Loder and his companion moved.

It was nearing one o'clock, and the Café of Clouds was beginning to reach its high spot of the evening. The pseudo-Hawaiian was finishing her dance, and from a cleverly con-cealed opening in the floor two lines of girls, dressed—in parts—to resemble the stars of the heavens, were moving gently towards the tables, amongst which they twirled dexterously and sinuously. The lights faded gradually until only silhouettes and sparkling gems were visible. With a steadily increased swell of music a glow of blue light spread upwards from the floor. The Queen of the Clouds was coming.

The hum of talk was hushed. For this moment the whole gathering had been waiting; the Queen of the Clouds possessed a voice purer by far than any that could be heard in musical comedy. Her head, crowned with a waving, swaying, voluptuous mass of feathers, appeared above the level of the floor. Her lips were parted.

High above the music, which had softened slowly, came a sharp report of a shot. A man in evening dress gurgled queerly, and slipped from his chair into the circle of light which was being spread over the Queen of the Clouds, an ugly stream of red running from an ominous hole in his forehead.

For a second there was no sound in the room. Then a woman screamed, a man called stridently for lights, and a dozen chairs scraped the floor. Near the door a girl fainted and collapsed, sending a small table over, to the crash of breaking glass.

Quinion was the first man to reach the body on the floor, and a name was hurling itself against the confines of his mind.

'Loder . . . Thomas Loder. . . .'

8

HELP FROM AUNT GLORIA

QUINION did not need more than a glance to see that
Loder was dead. The bullet had pierced his brain,
and death had been instantaneous. He made way quickly
for the manager of the Café of Clouds, and went to the side
of Miss Margaret Alleyn.

She was deathly white. The lights had been switched on
immediately, and her eyes were expressionless. Quinion had
to jerk her arm before she looked at him without recognition; and his fingers touched something hard and cold
which was laying near her hand. His own hand closed over
it quickly and he slipped it into his pocket. He felt his heart
beating more quickly than it should. What was that revolver
doing on the table, as though dropped from Margaret
Alleyn's fingers?

Quinion knew that the only chance of getting out of the
Café lay in moving quickly. A number of half-scared men
and women were already making a crush at the doors; at any
minute the police might arrive to force everyone back in
their places. Pulling an opera cloak round the girl's shoulders, he supported her with his arm, making grimly for the

door. Before they reached it, Margaret Alleyn seemed to come out of the trance into which she had fallen. Jimmy felt her body stiffen and heard the sudden intake of her breath.

'Push hard!' he said tersely.

She glanced towards him, and he caught the look of recognition which sprang into her eyes. There was no trace now of the stupor, and she realized the urgency of the need for escape.

They were through the door when Quinion saw two blue helmets towering above the crush of diners-out, and heard the gruff: 'Keep back, there, keep back, no one's to go out.' He looked round desperately, catching the eye of a waiter who beckoned him with a barely perceptible nod. A five-pound note changed hands, the waiter motioned them to follow him, and within three minutes the Hon. James and the girl were being rushed into a taxi, which moved off quickly.

Leaning back on the cushions, neither the man nor the girl spoke for several seconds, and it was not until Quinion had stopped the taxi and had a brief talk with the cabby that he broke the silence. In the dim light the profile which he had admired against the blue background of the sky over the Sussex Downs seemed to possess an added beauty.

'It serves to prove,' he said lightly, 'that the regulations are justified in objecting to the lights being turned down.'

She responded with a ghost of a smile.

'Yes, doesn't it?' She moved towards him suddenly, and he caught a wave of perfume. Her voice, still husky, was filled with urgency. 'Mr. Quinn, you are putting yourself on the wrong side of the law by doing this. . . .'

Quinion chuckled and patted her hand.

'It isn't the first time—it probably won't be the last—and there certainly won't be a better cause.'

Her smile came more naturally.

'I suppose that it's all a matter of practice?'

She glanced towards the Egyptian cigarette that he was smoking. Hastily, he threw it out of the window.

'Part of my up-to-London rig-out,' he said humorously. 'My pomade is nearly as bad too. It's all a matter of . . .'

'Practice?'

'I was going to say "habit",' retorted Jimmy, 'but it amounts to the same thing, and beyond a temporary irritation, it doesn't amount to a great deal. But let us talk of more important things.'

She took in a deep breath, as though squaring her shoulders for what was coming.

'You mean Loder?'

'I mean nothing of the kind,' replied the Hon. James with decision. 'It's far too late, and I'm far too tired for discussion about him. He'll do in the morning. No, I mean you.'

She looked at him levelly.

'Just how, Mr. Quinn?'

'What do you propose doing to-night?' he inquired.

'I don't know. With Loder I would have gone back to Runsey, but . . .' she sank back with a gesture of weariness. 'I don't know,' she repeated. 'Everything has got out of hand. . . .'

'The very words that I used myself earlier in the evening. The thing is, are you prepared to let me try to get them back?'

'How can you? You know nothing of Loder, nor my father. The business has been going on for years. I shall just have to let it work itself out.'

'Rome wasn't built in a day,' he said, 'but it was burnt in a night. A large young man with plenty of practice at throwing

54

people about can do all kinds of unexpected things. What I want you to do is to place yourself unreservedly in my hands. After we've had a little chat in the morning, forget as much as you can of Loder and his "business"; remember that queer things happen in this world, but they usually turn out brighter than they look like doing. For instance, I don't always smoke Egyptian cigarettes.'

Margaret smiled obediently.

'What is it you want me to do?'

'This is how I've been thinking,' said Jimmy. 'At Runsey Hall I have a perfectly angelic aunt who simply glories in looking after young and beautiful maidens who are worrying about something that has got out of hand. Come with me there, keep pretty close indoors for a few days, and let me tackle Oak Cottage. If you like, I'll exchange notes with you occasionally. It isn't too terrible a proposition, is it?'

She brushed her hair back from her forehead with another gesture of weariness which yet held a hint of relief.

'It sounds heavenly!' she admitted. 'But why should you put yourself out, Mr. Quinn?'

Quinion smiled. Margaret Alleyn felt the warm blood rushing to her cheeks under the close regard of his flecked grey eyes.

'Because I have a foolish, unreasoning desire to hear you call me "Jimmy",' he said, 'and I couldn't very well ask Aunt Gloria to look after someone who only knew me as Mr. Quinn—could I?'

It was approaching five o'clock, and the early grey light of dawn was spreading across the sky when the taxi turned into the drive of Runsey Hall. Quinion, after a hurried consultation with the taxi-driver, ushered the girl into a room which contained, amongst other things, a luxurious settee.

He saw her comfortably settled against the yielding cushions, spread a rug over her legs, and grinned gaily.

'Welcome to Runsey,' he said. 'Now I'll have a look in the cook's quarters and search for tea—or would you prefer coffee?'

Assured that her preference was for tea, he went into the hall, collected the cabby, who was staring in fascination at a large oil painting which by reason of its 'back to nature' movement, would have shocked the susceptibilities of his suburban-minded spouse, and made for the kitchen. As a bachelor he was not unacquainted with brewing tea and slicing bread-and-butter—although he held doubts of his ability to cut the latter thin enough for the enjoyment of a delicately nurtured maiden, but he was incurably optimistic—and the cabby demonstrated his domestic training by grilling bacon and frying eggs to perfection. Glowing with justifiable pride, the two men carried their spoils into the presence of the girl; and the Hon. James was once more convinced of the wisdom of optimism.

9

WHO SHOT LODER?

'I'VE told her,' said Quinion, smiling into the eyes of
Lady Gloria Runsey, 'that you are, bar none, the most
angelic angel on earth. Mind you live up to it.'

Lady Gloria smiled back.

'I'll look after her, Jimmy. I'm glad . . .'

'Finish it!' commanded Quinion sternly.

'I'm glad that you seem to have adopted a serious purpose in life.'

Quinion grinned.

'One wonders whether the great Colonel Damn, knowing the full circumstances, would approve. They might even
shock you,' he added. 'You see, I am officially on holiday.'

A cloud, which might have been of apprehension,
chased the smile from Lady Gloria's eyes. For a long time
she had had suspicions of the nature of her nephew's frequent 'holidays' from England, a suspicion which had been
engendered after he had returned from one five weeks' trip
abroad, swathed in bandages which were officially the results
of a motor accident. 'But why,' Lady Gloria had demanded

of herself, 'did none of the papers mention the accident?' For the Hon. James Quinion, she knew, was 'news' for the most conservative gossip columns. On the previous day Jimmy had given her a guarded hint that his activities during these excursions were not solely the 'wine, women and perdition' efforts in which Colonel Cann, his uncle, firmly believed.

Quinion saw the sudden change in her expression, and placed one hand beneath her chin.

'There's positively nothing to worry about—providing you keep Margaret near the Hall,' he said.

He went from the large, sun-lit room to his own bedroom. A short, thin, sombre-looking man, dressed in black, smiled a welcome.

'Good morning, sir. Will you have the blue, the grey, or the silvers, Mr. Quinion?'

'None of them,' said Jimmy definitely. 'I'm going to wear those trousers and that coat which you wanted to burn five years ago, Tally, and if I ever catch you trying to smuggle them out again I'll punch your nose.'

Augustus Tally, Quinion's devoted but often disapproving valet endeavoured to smile, but failed. From the hidden depths of a vast wardrobe he brought forth the disreputable garments and laid them out, his white fingers touching them gingerly.

'Very good, sir.'

'You're an old hypocrite!' said Quinion calmly. 'You don't think it's very good at all; you fancy that if I wear those togs more than once a year I'm sinking rapidly in degeneration and what-not. Don't you?'

'I have seen you in clothes which are more *fitting*, sir.'

'But not more comfortable. Comfort is one of the few things worth worrying about in this wicked world. However, let us end the discussion. Find out whether Miss Alleyn, who is in the blue room, sleeping off the effects of my eggs-and-bacon, is showing any signs of recovery, and ask her whether she's fit enough for the sight of me. She calls me Jimmy, but if you don't feel up to that you can say "Mr. Quinn".'

'Yes, sir,' said Tally, without enthusiasm.

'Then hurry!'

Augustus Tally moved soberly towards the door and closed it behind him.

It was nearing twelve o'clock, six hours and more since the oddly assorted trio had made their impromptu meal. Quinion had not slept for long, however; he possessed a useful facility of being able to manage without sleep for long periods, and it had often served him well. He had been into Runsey, seen the man named Smith, who was but slowly recovering from the effect of his meeting with the two men—being Reginald Chane and Peter de Lorne, who had introduced themselves exuberantly as 'sent by Archie'—and who was inclined to doubt whether he was safer with them than with Thomas Loder.

Quinion assured him that he was much safer with Loder. 'You see,' he had said briefly, 'Loder is dead.'

He had plunged into an account of the happenings at the Café of Clouds, omitting the incident of the automatic which he had taken from the table, and endeavouring, as he talked, to straighten the whole affair out in his mind.

It was then that he recalled a fact which had made him stop suddenly in the middle of his story.

During the whole of the disturbance at the Café of Clouds the music had continued to play!

As he walked across the downs from the Tavern to Runsey Hall—the three men at the Tavern were to watch events at Cross Farm and Oak Cottage and to telephone him should anything untoward happen—he had turned that recollection over in his mind.

He admitted that he was willing, over-anxious, perhaps, to build up a story that would free Margaret from any suspicions of having shot Thomas Loder. It was difficult. Her temporary stupor, the little revolver near her hand—on its silver handle he had found the initials 'M.A.' much to his dismay—and the general circumstances, all suggested that she had fired the shot. She had motive, too. Quinion was quite sure that she hated Loder, and yet she had been forced by some reason that obviously concerned her father, to put up with his company. On top of which there was the dark fact that in the dimly lighted Café of Clouds, no one who was not close to the dead man at the time of the shooting could have directed a shot with such accuracy.

It was, Quinion thought, a very black outlook. His chief hope was that the police—he did not doubt but that they were investigating the affair thoroughly—would not learn of Margaret Alleyn's connection with the victim of the affair.

Another point which puzzled Quinion was the dual identity of Margaret as the 'latest thing' from New York. From de Lorne he had learned that she was appearing in a minor part, and that she had only been in the show for two or three days. He hoped that the girl herself would explain her appearance on the stage. Her name, de Lorne had said, was shown on the bills as 'Elise Farily'.

Quinion was arrayed in his sports jacket and ghastly trousers when Augustus Tally returned.

'Miss Alleyn is awake, sir. She will be ready in twenty minutes.' The man's expression suggested that the estimate was optimistic; he had, apparently, ideas on the time which it took young women to dress.

'I take it that someone has looked after clothes and things?' Quinion said. 'Miss Alleyn's visit was unpremeditated; moreover, it is unnecessary to discuss it with the lads of the village; you might inform the other servants about that, will you?'

'I will give instructions, sir. Regarding wearing apparel, Lady Gloria has instructed Alice to wait on Miss Alleyn, Mr. Quinion.'

'Quick work,' said Jimmy. 'Right you are, Tally—oh——'

'Sir?'

'About hair oil. How much have I got?'

'You had a fresh consignment on July the twenty-first. There are about eleven bottles remaining.'

'I was going to leave it to you in my will,' said Quinion, 'but I think you might as well have it without waiting. Don't let me see any of it again. And then there are Egyptian cigarettes. . . .'

'Yes, sir.'

'How many millions of them are left?'

'Ten boxes of five hundred.'

'As a matter of fact,' said Quinion confidingly, 'I fancy that they're not being appreciated by the people who matter. I was going to bequeath them to you too, but you can have 'em when you like. Get me some Virginia 3's, and a fresh stock of Edgeworth for the briar.'

'Very good, sir,' said Tally, who was not overwhelmed by his employer's sudden generosity. He was at the door when Quinion called him back.

'One little condition, Tally, is that you mustn't smoke those cigarettes in my presence. I might fall from my high resolve if you tempt me.'

A little more than twenty minutes later he was sitting at a small table on the lawn of Runsey Hall, lunching contentedly with Margaret Alleyn.

The girl showed little traces of her all-night journey and the killing of Thomas Loder. Quinion made no mention of the latter until lunch was all but finished. Then, smoking a Virginia 3, he regarded his companion with a half-quizzical, half-serious gaze.

'And now, Margaret—as a matter of fact,' went on Quinion, 'I'm going to call you "Gretta"; it sounds more friendly. However, we can't dilly-dally round last night's affair too long; people are liable to start asking questions.'

He saw her sudden apprehension.

'It isn't worth worrying about yet. Loder was poisonous, and the police know it, but they'll also want to know who killed him. Now—before you speak, I want to tell you that if the authorities knew that I had found this gun with one barrel empty, they would want to know where.'

Margaret was staring wide-eyed at the dainty-looking automatic with a silver butt that Quinion was holding in his hand; there was no question but that she recognized it as her own. Yet her response was composed; and Quinion believed that, having once gained control over her emotions, she would not slip back easily into the state of collapse.

'Where was it?' she asked.

Quinion slipped the gun back into his pocket.

'On the table at which you and Loder sat,' he said quietly, 'close to your hand.'

There was a silence which lasted for a full minute. The girl was obviously working it out in her own mind; and Quinion could have sworn that there was no suggestion of guilt in the expression of those clear, deep hazel eyes.

'Which means,' she said finally, 'that I would have a difficult task in convincing anybody that I knew nothing about the shooting.'

'More than difficult,' Quinion said.

'And you?' The question shot out so quickly that it took Quinion unawares. The glowing brown eyes were fixed on his, almost challenging.

'I am quite convinced that you did not shoot Loder, but I'm not sure that you know nothing about the shooting, nor that you are ignorant of the name of the man—or woman— who did kill him.'

There was another tense silence, which the girl broke slowly.

'What makes you so sure that I—did not?'

Quinion puffed a cloud of grey smoke towards the smiling blue sky. They might, from appearances, have been talking of anything but the murderous topic of a cold-blooded killing. The late September air held a peaceful serenity.

'You were sitting with Loder and looking, as he was, towards the Queen of the Clouds. He was shot full-face. It was impossible for you to shoot him from the angle at which you were sitting. I think that that one fact is convincing, besides which'—he stared at her straightly— 'I am not prepared to believe that you shot him . . . even if the evidence was a lot more damning!'

The expression in her eyes might have been of relief, or gratitude, or of satisfaction; Quinion believed that it was a combination of all three.

'Thank you,' she said simply. 'I did not shoot Loder.'

'Splendid!' Quinion said. 'I've been waiting for that assurance since last night. But . . .'

She leaned forward.

'But what?'

'I still think,' opined Quinion, 'that you're a long time calling me Jimmy. However . . . these things take time. There's another little matter that we have to touch on. . . .'

'And that is?'

'Who did kill Loder?' demanded Quinion.

10

TALK OF THE MISER

FOR a third time a silence fell over the luncheon table, but it remained unbroken for much longer than before. Quinion smoked steadily, convinced that he would learn all that Margaret could tell him of the affair in which she had become entangled, and prepared to wait until she had sorted the story out in her own mind. He spent a few minutes in asking himself for an explanation of his own attitude where it concerned the girl.

He was not, as has been seen, an unsophisticated man. He belonged to that stratum of society which had every possible assistance for the search for beauty and which achieved that beauty in no small measure. Being eligible, there had been many occasions when he was compelled to flee from the cloying company of otherwise charming young women. Not that he had always elected to fly; he was by no means impervious to charm; but hitherto his interest had been much in the nature of his interest in musical comedy; that of a sometimes enthusiastic but sometimes, and more often, completely bored spectator. His main enthusiasm had been reserved for his efforts as Number 7 in the organization of Department 'Z'.

Now, however, in spite of his better judgment, he found himself regarding the safety and security of Margaret Alleyn the most important matter in his life.

He did not, because he could not, endeavour to explain it to himself; it had become a fact of paramount importance, and he had accepted it as such, for which reason he had offered Gordon Craigie his resignation and shown his mind with no uncertainty to Lady Gloria, the man named Smith, Reginald Chane and Peter de Lorne.

Watching the expressive face in front of him he smiled. A brief day before he would have scoffed at the idea; now . . .

Margaret drew in her breath, once again creating the impression that she was squaring her shoulders. Quinion's smile became more encouraging.

'All set?'

She flashed a smile, yet Quinion thought he detected a trace of disquiet. He made no comment, however, and the girl spoke quietly.

'I don't know who actually killed Loder,' she told him, 'but I do know who was behind the shooting. At least——' She broke off with a short laugh, before she went on: 'I know him by reputation. Mr. Quinn.'

'Jimmy.'

'Well . . . Jimmy . . . It's so terribly complicated that I don't know where to begin. It's . . .'

'Supposing I ask a few leading questions. Will that help?'

'It might.'

'There's nothing like being non-committal,' said Quinion. 'We'll have a shot at it. How long have you known Loder?'

'Six months,' answered Margaret.

'Had you heard of him before you met him?'

'Yes—at least, father spoke of him often.'

'How long had your father known him?'

'Five . . . nearly six . . . years. From the time that he was crippled.'

'Has your father spoken of Loder during all that time? Or did you hear of him later?'

'So far as I know he told me after the first time they had met.'

'That means that your father had known Loder since the fellow came from Canada. Now . . . have the two men always been good friends?'

'Well'—Margaret hesitated for a moment before answering uncertainly— 'I would hardly call them that. They had nothing in common apart from business, and each seemed afraid that the other would steal a march. . . .'

'Hum,' commented Quinion again. 'Then we can say that they were anything but good friends.' He leaned forward suddenly and spoke with an earnestness which robbed his words of all offence. 'Gretta—I may seem impertinent, but this affair has turned badly for you. What *is* this business between your father and Loder?'

He realized that she had been preparing for the question, and he hated the need for forcing it. She was playing with a knife, obviously unable to keep her hands from trembling.

'Jimmy . . .' The name came out naturally, and seemed to possess a wealth of appeal. 'It has only been during the last six months—since I met Loder—that I have known that before his illness my father traded in stolen gems.' She broke off, eyeing Quinion anxiously to see the effect of her words. He did not seem unduly disturbed. In fact, he was smiling, a soft, consoling smile.

'One of the nicest fellows I've ever met,' he said quietly, 'made his fortune out of the same game. It's just another method of looking at the social system.' He grinned suddenly. 'His two sons are at Oxford now, and their father's one great desire is that they never learn about his calling. *They* are happy enough; why shouldn't *you* be?'

Her hazel eyes glowed for a moment, giving him all the thanks he needed. He shifted uncomfortably when she spoke.

'I wonder if I shall ever be able to thank you enough for what you are doing.'

It was impossible to tell her just how much he wanted to help, for it would tell unmistakably of lack of control; moreover, it would prevent him from maintaining the attitude of independence which he knew he would have to adopt while dealing with the relationship between father and daughter. He covered his thoughts with a smile which became more confident.

'There isn't the slightest need for thanks,' he assured her. 'I could back out if I wanted to, but life has given me an inquisitive turn of mind . . . so I'm still in the hunt. Now, let me get things straight.

'You first heard of Loder six years ago, after your father had been crippled, but it was not until you met poor Thomas that you knew of the "business" between them. I take it'—he spoke slowly, smiling the while— 'that Loder used the fact of your father's activities to make you accept him as a friend?'

She answered him frankly:

'Yes. And I detested him.'

'Splendid!' said Quinion approvingly. 'Now. Were stolen jewels the extent of the activities of Loder? And of your father?'

She hesitated this time, and he smoked quietly, giving her the opportunity to arrange her thoughts.

'No . . . I don't think so. You see, during the last six months, while Loder has been at Cross Farm, both of them have been afraid of something more than interference from the police. Otherwise Loder would not have kept a dozen or more men at the Farm . . . and I know that all of them use revolvers. Once, when I was at the Farm, Loder was scared of something; all the doors were locked, the windows fastened, and men were stationed all about the house with instructions to shoot if necessary.

'Then, two or three days ago, one of the men mutinied. He escaped from the Farm, but Loder knew that he had not got far away. It was the man who was killed yesterday.'

She pressed one hand against her forehead. Quinion needed no telling of the effort that she was making. For months past she had been unable to escape from the influence of Loder, and she had realized, gradually, the nature of the man and something of the plans that he had on foot. An ordeal enough to have made any girl give way under the strain. Yet—he hated himself for admitting the thought—mightn't she have made some effort to get away? After all, there were limits to the duty owed to a father who failed in his.

She leaned forward suddenly, almost as though she had read his thoughts.

'It's been quite damnable! Two months ago I ran away; within three days Loder had found me. I tried again, but it was useless. For the past week or two . . . I have been afraid, literally afraid, to move from the cottage without asking permission. The little man who shot at you from the window has followed me everywhere.'

There was a hard expression in Quinion's flecked grey eyes as he listened. Loder had already paid . . . but Mr. Arnold Alleyn and Funny Face remained to answer for their treatment of the girl. He leaned forward, covering her small hand with his.

'Damnable is the word,' he assured her. 'But you can forget about it now. Loder's gone. I'll look after the little man, and your father. . . .'

He stopped suddenly. Her eyes held stark fear, yet she spoke evenly.

'Yes, my father. I am more frightened of him than of any of the others. Loder used to think that he was the leader, but he never has been. That was the cause of the trouble between them. Recently, since Loder has been bringing his "friends" to the Cottage and father has taken part in their discussions, Loder realized that the men were taking more notice of father than of him. I've known that one or the other would have to die.' She broke off with a gesture of great weariness, and it was several minutes before she resumed lifelessly. 'Mr. Quinn . . . I warned you that Loder was dangerous, but compared with my father he was a toy. . . .'

Quinion stood up. About them a gentle breeze played softly, and fifty yards away Aunt Gloria was gazing peacefully on to the world which she knew only as a spectator. By the window a Sealyham puppy played frivolously with a staid Scotch terrier, and behind a hedge a gardener whistled a haunting melody as he worked. Peace hovered in the garden. Yet at the table there was talk of death and fear and hate.

'Gretta,' Quinion asked quietly, 'can't you let yourself relax, here, and leave everything else to me?'

He knew her answer even before she spoke.

'No, it's useless. I've known for a long time that father thinks me too dangerous, that I know too much for safety. I believe that it was only Loder who stopped him from killing me, too. . . .' Her tone was so low that Quinion could scarcely hear her words, but suddenly she took on a new firmness. 'Don't you see, Jimmy, that if I stay here I'm bringing you into danger? I'm not imagining things. I *know* that father will stop at nothing. If I'm in his way, he'll get rid of me; if you are, he'll get rid of you. I can't stay here. I wouldn't be safe, and . . . *you* wouldn't; the only chance is for me to get out of England; and I can't do that. . . .'

Quinion sat down again, lighting his pipe and letting the match burn down to his fingers, watching it reflectively. Suddenly:

'You can get out of England just as soon as you want to, Gretta. Aunt Gloria is going to the South of France within two weeks; she would love to have you with her. Please leave it to me. But I shall have to know all that you know about your father.' He hesitated for several seconds before going on. 'From what I can gather, you think that he had something to do with the killing of Loder.'

'Yes, I do. But I don't think he was the main factor. There is someone else.'

'Who?'

She leaned forward, her attitude almost one of challenge. Quinion thought that he had never seen her more beautiful.

'It seems madness,' she told him quietly. 'It *is* mad. But . . . lately, as I told you, a number of "friends" have visited father and Loder. Most of them have been foreigners. Some of them have seemed important men, prosperous and influential. All of them have been either rich or clever.'

'Ten days ago four of them came together, and someone had to take notes of the meeting. They called me in.

'They spoke and acted just as if they were at an ordinary company meeting. The procedure was exactly the same; Father was elected acting-chairman, in view of the absence of the real leader, but they spoke of the other man sometimes, and always called him . . . The Miser.'

She looked across at Quinion as though half afraid that he would laugh, but his smile was sympathetic and understanding. Had she but known it, Quinion was used to hearing the most outrageous stories whilst knowing them to be perfectly true.

'I can't tell you much,' she went on. 'For all I could judge they might have been discussing a selling organization for butter and eggs. I had to make a list of names and addresses of men all over England, and type it out afterwards. That was all . . . except the way in which they always talked of the man called The Miser. They seemed afraid of him, Loder especially so. And once, when Loder was out of the room, one of them said that The Miser was attending to him. I can't explain it, but it was horrible. Whenever they mentioned the man who was absent it seemed to make me afraid. . . .'

So engrossed were they in themselves that they had not noticed the small car, containing three men, which had raced along the drive of Runsey Hall, coming to a stop fifty yards away from the table. Quinion's first realization of its arrival came with a shout from one of the men.

'Get under cover, Jimmy . . . run like hell!'

It was Reginald Chane. And his companions were Peter de Lorne and the man named Smith.

11

A Burglary at Oak Cottage

'JUST what is your latest little game, Reggie? Hide-and-seek?' Quinion demanded.

Reginald Chane had collapsed after his exertions and leaned back in a large arm-chair, murmuring pitifully for beer, opened his eyes a little and regarded the Hon. James reproachfully.

'Of course it isn't. I just wanted to see you run. I wondered whether you could.'

'I'm not sure,' said Quinion ferociously, 'whether I shall hit you on the head with a chair or just use my fist. Of all the crazy, maniacal, thoughtless, ill-timed jokes, this latest one of yours is the golden limit. What do you think, Gretta?'

Margaret was still breathing heavily after the sudden run from the lawn into the house, but the fear which had seized her for a few moments had been dispersed by Chane's bland assurance that the hoax had been successful. Her relief was so great that she could not share Quinion's righteous indignation. Consequently, she began to smile without answering.

'There you are,' said Chane. 'By her silence she tells the world that she enjoyed the joke. Jimmy, bow down and give me best . . . or call for some beer.'

Ten minutes later the four men were sitting in Quinion's room. The air was thick with smoke, and occasional silences were disturbed by the gurgling sound made by rich brown ale as it left its tankards and flowed smoothly down one or more eager throats. Quinion had just entered, and Reginald Chane was just finishing his third tankard.

'Not bad beer,' he said thoughtfully. 'Where'd you get it from, Jimmy?'

'I'm not going to tell you,' said Quinion, with decision. 'They don't brew enough to keep you going, guzzler, and I'm damned if I'm going to risk losing my only beverage because you're a hog. I've put the girls in the library,' he said irrelevantly. 'It's a room without windows.'

De Lorne choked suddenly, juggling madly with his tankard. He emerged triumphant, placing the tankard reverently on the table.

'I'll have to tell Aunt Gloria,' he said engagingly, 'that you called her a girl. She'll be more convinced than ever that you're crazy, Jimmy, although from the number of years she's nursed you I fancy she's pretty near sure. However——'

'However has it,' said Quinion. 'Now tell me what the trouble is.'

De Lorne pointed towards the man named Smith, who was leaning back in his chair, still unaccustomed to the near-insane irrelevancies of the man called Archie and his friends.

'Ask him,' said Peter. 'He's got more time. You'll have to teach him how to drink beer, Jimmy. Apart from that weakness he's almost human.'

'Such praise,' said Quinion, 'is praise indeed, Smithy, but don't let it go to your head. What made you rush up here?'

The man named Smith smiled.

'I thought, once, that it was because of a word that we heard from the little fellow you called Funny Face; but I'm not sure now that it wasn't because de Lorne knew you kept good beer.' He became serious, eyeing Quinion with those strangely clear blue eyes. 'Say, Quinn, I've a guess that whoever is in charge of Cross Farm, now that Loder's been bumped off, believes that you've got the girl up here. Chane thinks so too. I was strolling round the Farm keeping my ears open and eyes fixed, when I saw Funny Face and a guy he called Chevvers. He was grumbling, thinking more about a game of poker than the job he'd been sent out on. Someone—I couldn't find out who—had given him instructions to watch Runsey Hall for any signs of Miss Alleyn. I cut across to the Tavern and found that Chane had just arrived, having heard the same story. We all rushed out here.'

'Thinking,' interrupted de Lorne, 'that you'd want to keep her out of sight.'

'For once you thought right,' said Quinion. 'But was it necessary to raise a scare like that? And did you have to chase up here in Smithy's car, telling the world that you were worried about something?'

De Lorne lifted a paper-weight thoughtfully.

'If you got what you're asking for, Jimmy, you'd have this at your head. Yes, it was necessary. Not a hundred yards down the road we passed Funny Face and Chevvers, and we couldn't have got you and the girl to move mighty quick with ordinary persuasion. It would have looked suspicious, and worrying for her. The way we did it might have made us look kindergarten, but it did save a lot of explanation, James.'

'Not bad,' conceded Quinion.

'For the other matter,' said de Lorne, 'it isn't Smithy's car. It's one that Reggie and I hired from the local garage. We fixed it by telephone, and paid in cash through the pot-boy at the Tavern. Which made sure that no one but the pot-boy *knew* who'd hired it, and he won't have a chance to talk until the car's day of usefulness is over. And to make quite sure that no one knew Smithy was mixed up in the speeding, we made the poor blighter duck down at the back. We heard him swearing all the way. And if you still feel like teaching me how to hoodwink a gang of thugs, my lad, I'll throw this paper-weight at you; if that's not heavy enough, I'll try the tankard.'

'All right,' said Quinion. 'When the others aren't here, Peter, I'll tell you where I get this beer.' He dropped his bantering tone suddenly, and the smile in his eyes reflected the depth of his friendship for de Lorne and Chane, both of whom had been co-opted several times as temporary members of Department 'Z'. 'I'll arrange to keep Margaret inside the house until we're clear of Funny Face and his friends. Then I'll have another look at Oak Cottage myself; there are interesting things about Arnold Alleyn, unless I'm greatly mistaken.'

Two hours afterwards Quinion and Reginald Chane approached the outwardly heavenly Oak Cottage. Quinion had learned from Margaret that there was a passage leading from Cross Farm to her own home, and which opened into the office, the floor of which was operated on a sliding sys-tem and could be opened or closed at a moment's notice. It had been on the building of the passage and the floor that most of the men in Loder's employ had been engaged.

The girl knew little or nothing of the places in which her father kept the papers which Quinion was sure existed, but Quinion, having been given a clear run by Gordon Craigie, determined to make as thorough an investigation of Oak Cottage as he could.

In spite of his manner, he was not taking the affair lightly. Gordon Craigie, a man who never allowed himself to be fooled into believing a small affair serious, had stressed the importance of the association which Loder had been working up with Arnold Alleyn. The man named Smith had spoken of the visits which Loder had made to the continent, and Margaret had talked of the callers at the cottage, all rich or clever. Without question something was afoot which would, Craigie believed, aim a blow at the stability of England. If anything was needed to convince Quinion of the seriousness of the situation, he had had it when he had faced death at the end of a revolver whilst looking into the queer, light eyes of Arnold Alleyn.

They had mapped out a plan of campaign which in its very simplicity harboured success. Chane, unknown to Alleyn, would make an official call on the invalid, proclaiming himself a private detective working on behalf of the Café of Clouds, and making the fact of Alleyn's acquaintance with Loder the reason for his call. Quinion, meanwhile, would investigate the rear entrance of Oak Cottage.

'All of which,' said Quinion, as the two men separated about a hundred yards from the Cottage, 'might be very nice and handy; but on the other hand, Alleyn is a wise old bird, and may have some tricks up his sleeve. So keep a hold on your gun, Reggie, and if anyone shows their teeth, let 'em see you're not quite the fool you look. Good luck, my hearty!'

Quinion, skirting the cottage, smiled grimly when he saw the window through which he had hurled the chair boarded up with pieces of plain wood. There was no one about, from what he could judge, and he hoped that most of the men from Cross Farm were either at the Farm itself or keeping an eye on Runsey Hall in the hope of catching sight of Margaret. De Lorne and the man named Smith were still at the Hall.

The garden at the rear of the cottage was scrupulously tidy. It was fenced round with six feet of high slatted wood, topped with several strands of barbed wire which helped to make the fence an awkward but not an insuperable obstacle. A hedge which ran across the garden, separating the flowers from the more domestic vegetables, could serve as temporary cover if necessary, and a toolshed might afford a similar harbour. Quinion had seen many worse places for marauding excursions.

He had learned from Margaret that the only servant at the Cottage was a woman who came in during the mornings. All the food was cooked at Cross Farm and brought through the subterranean passage to the Alleyns. There was no fear of discovery from servants; the only trouble lay in the possibility of Alleyn having placed a guard inside the house. From the complete silence Quinion decided that it was unlikely; men of the type of Funny Face did better than to spend their time in silent communion with themselves.

He was further reassured when he found that the back door was locked; if a man had been stationed inside the kitchen, the locking of the door would have been unnecessary. Working quickly with a thin piece of wire, Quinion told himself that the chances of his getting away with a successful piece of burglary were good. When the lock clicked back and the door opened into an empty kitchen he permitted himself a smile.

JOHN CREASEY

From Margaret Alleyn he had learned the lay-out of the cottage. The kitchen opened into a small room which was used for meals, and which in turn led to the larger chamber in which he had been entertained on the previous afternoon. Part of the office, which he had also seen, was on the right of the small room and ran the whole length of the chamber in front. There were no doors saving those which led directly from one room to the next.

The door leading into the second and smaller room yielded to his touch. Placing his ear at the keyhole he heard a murmur of voices, obviously coming from the room beyond. Reginald Chane was doing his bit.

Only two pieces of furniture seemed to provide possible hiding places for papers. One, a small table with two narrow drawers, was filled with household bills and ordinary, every-day letters. Two minutes convinced Quinion that nothing of importance was in it. The second was a writing desk at which Alleyn, according to his daughter, did a great deal of his work, the office being used chiefly as a meeting place when more than one or two of the frequent visitors came. Quinion ran through the contents of drawer after drawer, satisfied that the papers which he examined contained nothing of importance. Only one drawer remained which had resisted his efforts to unlock.

He applied himself more seriously to it and felt it yielding, when a slight sound at his back made him swing on his heels. His hand was on his revolver in a flash, but his assailant was too close. Quinion felt a piece of lead piping thud sickeningly against the nape of his neck. A vivid flash of red flamed through his head before darkness came, followed by a roaring which dulled gradually as he sank into oblivion.

12

A Conversation at Oak Cottage

REGINALD CHANE spent an interesting half hour with Mr. Arnold Alleyn before deciding that it was time he went. Quinion would have finished any work that he had been able to do; in fact, Chane fancied that his friend and leader would probably be on his way back to Runsey Hall.

Reginald told himself that he handled the interview with commendable tact. Alleyn, although a little brusque at first, and careful not to commit himself at any time, had accepted Chane as the private detective from the Café of Clouds without once questioning the other's right to interrogate him. He had not, however, admitted any friendship with Thomas Loder. A business acquaintance, he said, but hardly a friend. The dead man—without speaking ill of the dead, of course—was hardly the type with whom he, Alleyn, would be likely to make friends. The detective would appreciate that, naturally.

Chane assured the other that it was quite obvious and opined that the Café of Clouds had been presumptuous in insisting on Mr. Alleyn being troubled. He would see that they apologized in writing.

Chane himself, although fully aware that Quinion made few mistakes, especially in his gallery of rogues, was inclined to wonder whether he had not slipped up this time. Alleyn seemed a harmless old man, probably round about sixty-five to seventy, Chane thought, and if his eyes, queerly light grey, were a little out of the ordinary, it certainly did not stamp him as a criminal. It was pitiful to see Alleyn grasping his chair with white, trembling hands as he propelled himself along. An invalid, and one who certainly did not have a great deal longer to live . . . and Quinion had an idea that he was a big man behind a particularly nasty gang of scoundrels. A crazy idea, Chane thought; Jimmy was certainly dealing strangely with this affair; the girl seemed to have turned his head.

Chane, keeping up a conversation with Alleyn as he thought, wondered about the girl. She was, without doubt, extremely beautiful; enough to turn any ordinary man's head all right, but he was by no means sure of her. She had been with Loder at the Café of Clouds, and had certainly not seemed a reluctant reveller. She was on the boards with a New York show which was notorious for actresses who loved the gay life of the stage. She had pitched the tale of woe to Jimmy Quinion, and it had caught the Hon. James napping. Damn it, would any man believe that this gentle, soft-voiced invalid held his daughter in constant fear of her life?

'Well,' he said aloud, 'I shall have to be going, Mr. Alleyn. I'm deuced sorry at having bothered you, but'— he smiled deprecatingly— 'you know how difficult it is to make sure that one is always on the right track, don't you? The Café of Clouds will suffer pretty badly as a result of this business, and the management is extremely anxious to straighten it out. They haven't a great deal of faith in the . . . police. . . .'

'Quite so,' said Mr. Arnold Alleyn softly. 'There's just one other little matter, though, Mr. . . . Chane did you say your name was?'

'Chane,' agreed Reginald, smiling a little stiffly. Was he mistaken, or had that soft voice held a steely tone? Something in Alleyn's expression chilled him. He was suddenly on the alert, watching the other closely, and fingering the butt of his revolver for reassurance.

'I'm wondering, Mr. Chane, how it is that you were foolish enough to come and see me without first learning that I am the owner of the Café of Clouds. . . .' He broke off, smiling as Chane broke in in amazement.

'The owner? You?'

'Yes,' said Alleyn. There was a steely edge to his voice. He looked a different man, younger by ten or fifteen years than Chane's first estimate. But it was towards the small, dull grey automatic that Chane's eyes were turned; held in Alleyn's hand, which was firm in spite of its delicate frailty, it covered him unmovingly. 'Yes, Mr. Chane. I would advise you not to take that revolver out of your pocket. At the moment it is half in and half out. Move your hand away and let it drop back . . . that's right. I have owned the Café of Clouds since it first opened; it is, in fact, a most profitable business venture, but the management does not employ private detectives. In fact, there is no need for them in this case . . . I know who killed Loder.'

For the first time since the situation had veered round, Reginald Chane displayed some signs of emotion. He frowned.

'I hope you're not lying, Mr. Alleyn.'

Arnold Alleyn smiled. It was unpleasant, like the smile of a man who has triumphed by foul means and is baiting the loser. The light eyes gleamed malevolently.

'There is no need for me to lie, because there will be no opportunity for you to pass the information on. I shall have you looked after just as your friend Quinn is being looked after.'

For a third time Chane broke in.

'Quinn, Mr. Alleyn? I don't seem to recognize the name. Now, be reasonable. . . .'

There was something very nasty about Alleyn's smile.

'I might,' he said silkily, 'express the pious hope that *you* are not lying. But I won't . . . because I *know* you are. I have had a report of your movements since you came down to Runsey, and I am perfectly well acquainted with your connection with Mr. Quinn . . . and the man who called here the other day and called himself Smith. . . .'

'Now look here,' said Chane, fighting for time. If Alleyn was telling the truth, Jimmy Quinion was at the same disadvantage as he was himself. What chances were there of turning the tables? Precious few, from what he could see, but the more time he had the more likelihood was there that something would turn up; Chane, after the manner of the Hon. James Quinion, believed in luck. One thing Jimmy could congratulate himself on; Alleyn spoke of him as 'Mr. Quinn', and it was improbable that he would have done had he known his true name of Quinion. 'Now look here,' he went on, 'I'll grant that you have caught me out, so to speak, but let's talk it over in a perfectly reasonable manner. . . .'

'I'm afraid,' said Alleyn softly, 'that I haven't time to talk anything over. Beyond telling you that both yourself and the interfering Mr. Quinn will have a long journey as soon as it is possible for me to arrange it thoroughly, I have nothing more to say. So'—his lips seemed to turn back, baring his teeth in an almost animal snarl which made Chane curse himself for imagining that this man was a harmless invalid— 'so, Mr. Chane, for the time being . . .'

'Weren't you going to tell me who killed Loder, Mr. Alleyn?' demanded Chane easily.

Alleyn was quiet for several seconds. He seemed to be striving to regain the control which he had lost for a moment whilst he had leered at the younger man. He became once more the white-faced, gentle-looking invalid, and his silky voice was almost a purr.

'Yes, I did intend going that far, but I won't; I'll keep it until later, when I can have a word with your friend Quinn. Have you known Quinn long?' The question was rapped out, obviously intended to take Chane by surprise.

'Known him long?' he inquired blandly. 'But I just assured you that I had never heard the name.'

Alleyn, swerving suddenly in his wheel-chair, stretched out his right hand and pressed a switch in the wall. Once more the sneer had made his face take on the appearance of an animal rather than a man, and once again, in spite of his *applomb*, Reginald Chane felt his spine prickle with darts of fear. God! Alleyn was a——

The silky voice broke the momentary silence.

'I'm afraid I have little faith in your veracity, Mr. Chane. I have already told you that I know of your acquaintance with Mr. Quinn . . . for the rest, I assure you that if you move your right hand a fraction of an inch nearer your pocket I will shoot you. . . .'

Chane raised his brows in a whimsical acknowledgment of defeat. He had been manœuvring to get his own automatic without risking a shot from that which Alleyn held steadily in his left hand; but the invalid possessed powers of observation out of keeping with his appearance. There was silence for a few seconds.

'What is going to happen now?' demanded Chane, apparently tiring of inaction.

The invalid smiled. He looked now just as he had looked when Chane had first seen him; a harmless, ailing old man.

'I am going to ask one or two of my friends to escort you to Cross Farm. You have heard of Cross Farm, Mr. Chane?'

Once more the question was rapped out, and once more Chane presented a blandly innocent front.

'Cross Farm? Now let me see . . . I believe I heard some-one mention it at the Tavern.'

'Congratulations,' murmured Alleyn. He chuckled, as though to himself. 'I am inclined to believe, Mr. Chane, that you are more used to expeditions of this nature than you make out.'

Chane waved his hand airily, seeing the other's fingers tighten about the automatic.

'And yet I told you that I am a detective, Alleyn. . . .'

'In the employ of the Café of Clouds?'

'You score there,' Chane admitted. The easy smile left his face and he leaned forward. Alleyn, sensing the change as well as seeing it, interrupted him.

'Well, Mr. Chane? You were about to say. . . .'

Chane hesitated, as though weighing up his words. Actually he had been working out the plan of action that he would adopt since Alleyn had first revealed the more dangerous side of his nature. His plan was not foolproof, but it held possibilities and would probably give both him and Quinion an hour or two more in which to act.

'I was about to say that you forget that I may have been engaged by someone other than the Café. Admitting that I erred in thinking that the least likely manner of awakening your suspicions, you must see that I *did* not come down here purely for the sake of butting in.'

Alleyn appeared to deliberate over this.

'You mean that you are working on some third party's behalf?'

'Exactly that.'

'Excluding Mr. Quinn?'

'To be quite frank,' said Chane, with a gesture that suggested his anxiety to stop fencing and to get to grips with the real situation, 'I have met Quinn. He is staying at the Tavern, and quite by chance I discovered that he is interested in Oak Cottage through a young lady.'

'Yes,' agreed Alleyn, 'I know that the young fool is concerning himself with my daughter.'

'That is what I understood,' admitted Chane. 'Naturally, when I found that he was anxious to learn what he could of your activities, I invited him to join up with me. My greater experience in matters of—shall I say diplomacy? —appealed to him. We decided to make a concerted effort.' He stopped again, laughing grimly. 'I'm afraid I had not expected to meet with such clever opposition, Mr. Alleyn.'

'It is never wise to dabble in matters of which you know nothing,' said Alleyn, fingering the wheel of his chair with the fingers of his right hand. 'On whose behalf are you working?'

There was no question of the anxiety that he showed. At least Chane had found a chink in the man's armour. He shrugged his shoulders.

'You can hardly expect me to tell you without covering myself. . . .'

'What do you want for the information?'

'What do I want?' Chane appeared to deliberate. 'Well, I want your assurance that I shall be allowed to go from here, together with Quinn.'

'Why with Quinn?' Alleyn's voice, as he asked the question, lacked the silkiness which had hitherto been a characteristic. The words were rapped out and the tone was harsh.

'Because I rather like the man, and I don't like the idea of leaving him at your mercy, simply because he is fool enough to mix himself up with matters that are beyond him.'

The invalid leaned back in his chair, but the long white fingers still held their grip on the small butt of his automatic, and Chane did not relish the idea of making another attempt to get to his own revolver. Alleyn appeared to be deliberating. When he spoke he seemed undecided.

'Supposing I agree, Mr. Chane, what guarantee have I that you will act in good faith?'

Chane pursed his lips.

'Well,' he said slowly, 'you have none, of course. But look at the situation from my point of view, Mr. Alleyn. I have been engaged, as an investigator, to discover what I can about the murder of Thomas Loder. Frankly, it is not my first murder case, but it is the first one in which I have been accosted with threats after the fashion of that gun of yours.'

'Then why carry a gun yourself?'

Chane shrugged.

'Simply as a precaution, and a means of persuasion. Look here, Mr. Alleyn, I've seen quite enough of this affair to want to get out of it with a whole skin. I am not, like Quinn, bent on a quixotic errand; I am in it for what I can get out of it, and my fees are not heavy enough to run the risk of getting shot. Let me go, with Quinn, and I give you my assurance that I shall make no further efforts to discover

who killed Loder, nor interfere with you in any way. It's to
our mutual advantage.'

Alleyn interrupted him suddenly.

'All right, Chane. I give you my word that both of you
will be sent from here, unhurt. Now, who is it that is so interested in Loder that he wants to discover the name of his
murderer?'

Alleyn was waiting on the other's reply. Chane could
see the anxiety which filled those queer, light eyes. It would
have to remain there for a while, he thought grimly.

'Come, Mr. Alleyn. You hardly expect me to act up to my
part of the bargain while Quinn is still wherever you have
hidden him, and I am still unable to get out of the range of
your automatic.'

Alleyn's eyes narrowed, and for a third time Chane saw
the sneer which disfigured a face that was, in repose, a picture of dignified old age.

'No, I suppose it is asking too much. In a few minutes
now several of my friends will be here. I will get them to
bring the man Quinn in. Meanwhile——'

He broke off suddenly, his head turned towards the door
of the office. Chane, pouncing on the opportunity for which
he had been waiting since Alleyn had first admitted to the
ownership of the Café of Clouds, had his own automatic out
of his pocket and directed towards the invalid before the
other had recovered from his momentary surprise. Chane's
eyes were fixed on the forefinger of Alleyn's left hand; at the
first suggestion of a movement, his own finger would press
the trigger of his automatic.

But Alleyn's fingers, hitherto firmly gripping his gun,
relaxed. His face, already pale, took on a deathly pallor.

While from behind the office door came the sound of a
woman singing. Her voice was miraculous in its mastery; the

silver notes might have been from the haven of a thousand nightingales, and yet again might have been from the flawless throat of one alone.

Chane, intent though he was on keeping Alleyn covered, had a hard job to stifle an ejaculation of amazement. He had heard that voice before; and there could only be one like it. . . .

It was the Queen of the Clouds!

13

QUINION HAS A STIFF NECK

THE Hon. James Quinion began by cursing the beer at the 'Clarion', but a few moments of hazy reflection convinced him that he had not spent the previous night at that haunt of London's favoured few, and he turned his attention alternatively to the Tavern, Peter de Lorne's flat and the Café of Clouds.

Arrived at the Café of Clouds he began to think more clearly. It was incredible that even a place which was ostensibly run to fleece the idle rich should risk unpopularity by selling a liquor which made an old hand of the nature of the Hon. James wake up in the morning with a head worse than anything else on earth; at least, Jimmy assured himself that it was so. He turned over, flinching as a sheet of pain flashed through his aching head. Where had he been last night?

Slowly it dawned on him that he was not in bed. First his shoe—an unusual item beneath the sheets—stubbed against a chair-leg; and no ordinary chair sleeps with its owner. Then his hand banged against a drawer which was open, with the papers once contained in it strewn about a table. Shoes, chairs and table . . . Quinion, gritting his teeth at the torture, opened his eyes. Never in all his life had he had a head like it.

He was too concerned with the throbbing in his head to show surprise when he found himself sitting on a hardwood chair in the room which he had entered burglariously sometime before. As the realization of events came back to him he wondered, still without surprise, at being allowed to sit, unbound, on the chair. He remembered swerving round as someone crept up behind him, and he remembered the sickening thud which had sent him to sleep. But why should he be left in the empty room unattended?

He allowed himself five minutes in which to give the throbbing a chance to settle before standing up uncertainly and looking round. The room was exactly as it had been before he had been knocked out; only the papers, strewn about the table—he could imagine that he had dropped the drawer as he had fallen unconscious—were out of place.

He felt in his pockets and smiled as he found that his automatic was there; no one had searched him, then. What had happened to make his assailant disappear? Returning to a semblance of his normal self he began to thank the great god of luck, only to be jerked back as he stumbled against a chair and made the throbbing in his head increase a hundredfold. Gad! What a head! If only he could douse it in cold water.

There was a tap, he remembered, in the scullery through which he had passed. Walking gingerly to the door, moving smoothly in order to prevent jarring his head more than necessary, he went to the tap, turning it full on and letting the cool water run where it would. After five minutes he felt a new man.

A glance at his watch told him that it was nearly six o'clock, more than an hour since he had left Reggie Chane. What had happened to Reggie? Had he fallen for it as easily as Quinion himself? And had he been comparatively free when he had awakened? Quinion found himself bewildered by the hundred-and-one questions which flashed into his mind. There was only one way to answer them: Oak Cottage would have to be more fully explored.

By all the rules of common sense he should make good his escape from the cottage while he could; he walked towards the door which led to the room in which he had first sat with Margaret Alleyn. His chief purpose was the discovery of Chane; it might be that his, Quinion's, comparative freedom was accidental, and Chane was in need of help. Quinion turned the handle of the door.

He stood there for a moment, surprised into stupefaction. From the room ahead came the sound of a woman's voice, lifted in song; and Quinion thought that he had never heard a voice more pure nor notes reached with less effort in spite of their flawlessness.

Never? What of the Queen of the Clouds?

He pushed the door gently, and darted back as a gruff voice warned him to keep away. He could see, through the inch-wide opening that he had made, the muzzle of a revolver pointed towards him, held in a lean brown hand which wavered not at all. After the first shock Quinion began to laugh, and as he laughed the revolver faltered and drooped towards the ground. Mr. Reginald Chane, his aristocratic face registering astonishment, annoyance and relief, pulled the door full open.

'Funny, isn't it?' he demanded.

'Funny!' gasped Quinion. 'Funny! Oh, my hat, my head! Funny!'

'That's right,' said Chane lugubriously, 'laugh. I don't mind; in fact, I like it.'

'For the love of Mike,' implored Quinion, gasping, 'shut off that damned gramophone and stop staring like a gargoyle. Go on. Hurry. Double. . . .'

He slipped gratefully into an arm-chair . . . the one which had sheltered him from Funny Face's bullets, and gazed hopelessly at Chane as the latter lifted the needle from the record that was revolving on the cabinet gramophone standing in the middle of the room. Chane, who had steeled himself to deal with a small army of men which he had expected to arrive at any minute from Cross Farm, took some time to recover his equanimity. Gradually he began to smile. Finally, he offered Quinion a cigarette, lit one himself, and sat in a companion chair to Quinion's.

'You haven't got such a thing as a nip of strong liquor, have you, Reggie?' Quinion asked.

'There's some whisky in that decanter,' said Chane, reaching out for a decanter which stood on a small table. Quinion put it to his lips, spluttered, coughed, and suddenly remembered caution.

'Sure it isn't doped?'

'Sure of nothing,' said Chane comfortlessly, 'but I took a swig myself twenty minutes ago, and I'm still looking at life.'

'Sounds all right,' admitted Quinion. He lit his cigarette thoughtfully before giving his friend a brief account of his effort in burglary. 'And what have you got to talk about?' he asked finally. 'Been spending a happy hour with that?' He pointed towards the cabinet in the middle of the room.

Chane regarded the gramophone with a friendly eye.

'As a matter of fact you and I owe a great deal to that plaything, Jimmy, but I'm damned if I know just how.'

'Tell me everything,' demanded Quinion. 'Especially the whereabouts of Arnold Alleyn. . . .'

'I haven't a notion,' confessed Chane. 'Let me start properly. I called on Alleyn with the story we'd fixed up, and was travelling splendidly when he outed me by saying that he was the owner of the Café of Clouds . . . that's right, jump. Of all the crazy stunts, sending me to that mad hatter without first making sure that the story was foolproof.'

'Even I don't know everything,' murmured Quinion.

'I could have told you that many years ago, James. Alleyn had me more or less where he wanted me. I stalled him off for a bit, but was just about to give the whole thing up as a loser, and take whatever he had coming, when I heard that voice . . . just as you heard it just now. Jimmy, it turned Alleyn to cheese. There he was, looking at me with those nasty eyes of his and handling a nasty little gun in a business-like method; then he just crumpled up.

'I expected to see the woman who was singing come in through the door there'—he pointed towards the office and Quinion nodded—'but a man at the window called my attention; a sceptic looking little blighter with a face like popcorn. He had a gun, though, and I had to move pretty smart to dodge him, until I, and he, discovered that his gun wasn't loaded. After that I made grimaces at him and sent him running like a hare towards the end of the garden. All this time, you will gather, the voice was singing, and I had my back to Alleyn and the door; I don't know why, but I fancied that there was no need to worry about Alleyn getting cross at that minute.' He stopped, eyeing Quinion steadily, and it was several seconds before he went on.

'Jimmy, believe it or not, when I turned round again Alleyn was gone, chair and all. There wasn't a sign of him. The door leading into the office was open, but I could hear nothing coming through. I walked across, not too quickly in case someone popped round the corner, and saw that the "woman" was a tinned one. But there was no one at all in the room.

'Feeling a bit on the jumpy side I kept my eyes open, but nothing happened. Catching sight of that decanter, I investigated and took a swig . . . being, I don't mind telling you, thoroughly in need of a freshener, Jimmy. That made me gay, for after taking another look round I decided to hear my fair rescuer again, brought the gramophone in here and set her going. Then you came.'

Quinion sat silent for some time. Everything that had happened since he had first met Thomas Loder added to the confusion of his mind. That a man of the stamp of Arnold Alleyn would crumple up at the sound of a record being played was as near incredible as any of the things that had puzzled him, but it was a fact; Chane, in spite of the whisky, was quite sober.

'When you were having a look round, didn't it occur to you to try the door through which I came in?'

Chane frowned.

'Yes. I did. I looked out of the front door, but there was no one about; then I tried the other joker. It was locked.'

'Locked?' Quinion's tone was incredulous. 'Damn it, I must have come in less than ten minutes after you had tried it, and it was open then. Sure you're not dreaming?'

'As sure as I'm here,' affirmed Chane. He was looking tensely towards the door of the office; then he looked at the window. Quinion, his brows arched in puzzlement, followed his friend's gaze.

'Listen,' said Chane constrainedly. 'When I first came in the window was boarded up; yet the boards weren't there when the man with the face looked through, but they're back again.'

'Go on,' said Quinion grimly. He was looking now at the door of the office.

'When I tried the door through which you came, it was locked; ten minutes later it was open. When I looked through that office there was no one there, and I carted the gramophone into this room, leaving the door open; *now the door is shut.* I'm not dreaming; I'm dead sure! When you came in you left your door open, *and that's shut too!* Yet neither of us has moved. . . .'

Quinion, grim-eyed, stood up. His revolver gleamed in his hand as he moved towards the front door of Oak Cottage, and tried the handle. As he had half expected, it was locked. He knelt down, intent on picking it with the wire he had used to unlock the drawers in Arnold Alleyn's desk, but after a minute's effort knew that it was hopeless. He turned round.

'My God!' he breathed fearfully.

For there was no sign of Chane, although the big armchair was standing just where it had been before he had walked towards the door.

14

A TRIP TO CROSS FARM

AFTER the first moment of consternation Quinion moved quickly towards the door of the office. He held no faith in the supernatural where Oak Cottage was concerned; queer things were happening, but there was a definite explanation of them. That a man of the size and nature of Reginald Chane could be spirited away without a sound or struggle took some believing, but Quinion knew it for fact; it was the culminating point of the queer things that Chane had noticed and remarked upon, the silent closing and locking of doors and the boarding up of the window.

The door leading to the office was still locked, and the door of the room from which Quinion had come was equally fast. With his revolver still held firmly in his hand, Quinion began to walk slowly round the room, examining the walls and the floor for an opening of some kind; for Chane had gone, and it was nearly certain that he had not gone through the doors or the window. Quinion, who had played with the idea before, wondered whether the great fireplace sheltered any secret.

The ability to dissociate himself from anything but the problem immediately in front of him was one of the secrets of Quinion's success with Department 'Z', and as he peered into the recess of the fireplace he had no thought in his mind save the need of discovering a way out of Oak Cottage; that he was in all probability being watched by more than one pair of eyes troubled him not at all.

If there was any opening, it was well hidden, for after five minutes Quinion could find nothing at all that might help him. He stepped back from the hearth, knocking his feet against a poker as he did so. For a second he stood still, frowning; something had happened as he had kicked that poker, but it did not dawn on him at once. Gradually his frown increased, and he stepped forward deliberately, kicking the irons in the fender.

He had not been imagining things. *He heard nothing at all as the poker and the tongs moved one against the other.* Where there should have been a clattering of steel on steel, there was silence!

Something akin to fear crept into his mind, and he felt the prickling hairs rise at the back of his neck. Nausea seemed to creep into his stomach, and he felt sick . . .

Deaf! . . .

Suddenly he shook his head, pulling himself together with a physical effort. There was no sense in submitting to the fear which had taken hold of him for a moment. Had he been face to face with anything tangible it would have given him an added zest for life, even though he was in danger of losing it; but this silent moving of one or more people about the cottage—for someone must have locked those doors and boarded that window—followed by the discovery that he could not hear, began to play on his nerves.

He threw back his head and laughed crazily, trying to restore his confidence, but the hollow echo inside his head, which was the only sound that came to him in spite of the boisterousness of that laugh, chilled him again. He wasn't dreaming, nor imagining things; he could hear nothing!

He admitted to himself that he was unnerved, and throwing himself into the chair in which Chane had been sitting, lit a cigarette. Unless he could gain control over himself he was asking for trouble . . . and trouble was near enough as it was. He eyed the decanter of whisky grimly.

'It tasted all right,' he thought, 'but if there wasn't some drug in the damned stuff, what the devil has come over me?'

He lit another match, watching the spurt of flame. It was uncanny, seeing everything as usual and yet hearing nothing when he should have heard the sounds accompanying ordinary actions. In a way, of course, it explained the apparent ghostliness of the locked doors, the boarded windows and the disappearance of Chane. But it failed to help.

Quinion laughed grimly, without the sudden tension that had hitherto seized him when he had done anything without hearing it. He was becoming accustomed to this deafness. He laughed again, still more grimly, and yet with a suggestion of ironic humour. The Hon. James Quinion, fully fledged agent of Department 'Z', was sitting in the front room of an English cottage with a revolver in his hand, yet absolutely unable to make head or tail of his position. He *might* be the cynosure of several pairs of eyes, but on the other hand, whoever had taken Chane away might have gone with him.

Whatever else, he was helpless; there was nothing he could do. . . .

He stood up suddenly. There were several things he could do. The fireplace, for instance, could be much more thoroughly examined, and the rest of the room too. If he could still find nothing, he could break through the boards at the window; any one of the stiff-backed chairs would prove serviceable enough to batter them down. The horrible discovery of his deafness had sent him, mentally, to pieces.

A quarter of an hour passed while he made a complete examination of the old-fashioned fireplace and the walls of the room. Nothing rewarded his efforts; if there existed a secret entry into the room it was cleverly hidden. With tight lips he turned his attention to the window. If he did manage to make a getaway, it would mean leaving Chane behind, but he reasoned that it was better to get clear and to make a fresh attack on the cottage with de Lorne and the man named Smith rather than to risk being caught in the same net as Chane. But why had he been left unmolested? His own comparative freedom was one of the strangest items of the whole affair.

Slipping his revolver into his pocket he gripped a stout oak chair with both hands. He had to smash his way out quickly, and one mighty crash at the boards which covered the broken window sent them flying into the garden. He climbed out, looked round the garden, and began to run towards the main road, about a hundred yards ahead.

At the road, he stopped running and began to walk rapidly. He was thinking fast. Many small things which had been puzzling him for some time past gained utterance in his mind. How was it, for instance, that he and Chane had been unable to hear the locking of the doors and the boarding up of the window and yet had been able to hear each other speak? He endeavoured to fix the precise moment at which he had first lost his power of hearing, but it was difficult, for he had, after discovering the disappearance of Chane, moved about the room as silently as possible. He might have carried on for half an hour or more, but for banging against the poker.

Dusk was falling, and there was little traffic on the road. It would take him another ten minutes to reach the Tavern, and he spent the time in working out a plan of campaign for the rescue of Reginald Chane.

He had little doubt that Chane had been taken from Oak Cottage to Cross Farm. He knew that there was an underground passage connecting the two places, and he imagined that Chane had been taken into the office, with its movable floor, and thence to the farm. The man named Smith, de Lorne and himself would have to make a sortie on Loder's home, but it would probably be wiser to get in touch with Gordon Craigie first. The chief of Department 'Z' had said that he was getting news in hour by hour; it might easily be that he had learned something that would help Quinion.

The first cottage in Runsey was in sight when Quinion saw a large grey Buick speeding towards him. The main road was anything but safe for high speeds through the village, and he eyed the car with interest; the driver must have been in a devil of a hurry to get to town, for twice he swerved dangerously to avoid a nasty patch of road.

Quinion flattened himself against the hedge as the car flashed by, and cursed himself for five minutes as he tore towards the village, bent on getting a car to follow in the wake of the Buick. He was cursing because, in ordinary circumstances, he would have punctured one at least of the rear tyres of the large car with his revolver when he had recognized the occupants of it, but a second amazing discovery had momentarily dazed him.

He had *heard* the engine of the car, and the grinding of the tyres on the gravel road!

The revelation, great though it was, could not make him anything but furious that he had blundered so grievously in letting the Buick get away without making some attempt to stop it. For at the rear of the car Mr. Arnold Alleyn was sitting, and next to him, leaning back as though unconscious, was Reginald Chane!

Afterwards Quinion reflected that he had taken little time to adjust himself to his new-found ability to hear, in spite of the effect that his deafness had had on him when he had first discovered it. He dashed through the bar of the Tavern without heeding the curious stare of the barmaid who called him, in frivolous moments, Archie.

Smith and de Lorne were both in the private room that they had hired.

'Am I glad to see you,' breathed Quinion, banging the door behind him. What speed can you get out of that bus you hired?'

'Sixty at a pinch.' Peter de Lorne showed no surprise at the sudden intrusion, although Smith was staring at Quinion uncertainly.

'Hopeless,' said Quinion breathlessly. 'Smith, what can you do in that Singer of yours?'

'Cruise at seventy, if you want it,' said the Canadian. He fought back a desire to ask a hundred questions. 'I might manage more. Do you want it?'

'Yes. Get it out of the garage and head it for London. Fill up with enough petrol to drive all night if needs be.'

Smith stood up, stuffed his pipe into his pocket and went out of the room. De Lorne, pouring out a peg of whisky, handed it to his friend.

'Take your time,' he said quietly. 'Trouble, Jimmy?'

Quinion took a gulp of neat whisky.

'Chane's gone. Alleyn's taking him towards London in a Buick that passed me doing eighty, some lout banged me on the back of the head, and . . . oh, damn all telephones!' He looked at de Lorne and grinned. 'Sorry, Peter. I'm all het up. Answer that confounded thing, will you?'

As de Lorne went to the telephone Quinion finished his whisky, diluting it this time with Polly, and following up with a cigarette. As he puffed the first cloud of grey smoke de Lorne turned round.

'Yours, James. Shall I tell them you're out?'

Quinion stood up.

'It might be worth hearing. Hold them on.'

The expression on his face as he put the receiver to his ear convinced de Lorne that it was certainly worth hearing. Quinion muttered a brief 'hold on a second' and motioned de Lorne for a chair. He sat down, resting the telephone on the table.

'Who's that?'

The crisp voice at the other end of the wire was unmistakably Gordon Craigie's. Department 'Z' had had some news, apparently. But the first question made Quinion grin, in spite of himself.

'Is the girl all right, Number Seven?'—names were never mentioned over the telephone when speaking to or from Victoria Nought. Craigie had gone further than usual in speaking of 'the girl'.

'Yes,' said Quinion.

'Good. Made any progress?'

'Been hit on the head,' said Quinion ruefully. 'Hard.'

Had he not been sure of the man at the other end, he would have thought that it was a ghost of a chuckle that came over the line. As it was, there was no mistaking the whispered 'good'.

'Heartless so-and-so,' said Quinion. But the call from Department 'Z' cheered him considerably, in spite of the memory of Reggie Chane's white, vacant face as he had lolled back against the cushions of the Buick.

Craigie's next words were spoken in a tone that said plainly that all banter was to be dropped.

'Number Seven, I want you to carry on strictly according to your first instructions. Do you understand?'

Quinion hesitated a second. That meant, of course, that he would have to watch Cross Farm, and it also meant that he would be unable, himself, to chase after the Buick.

'Ye—es. Will one man be enough? There's plenty to do.'

'What?' demanded Craigie shortly.

'One of my co-opted members has been spirited away,' said Quinion. 'He's gone with an invalid. . . .'

'I know. . . .' Quinion arched his brows at that brief statement from the other end, but he had little time to think about it as Craigie went on: 'A Buick sedan smashed eight miles from you. The two men at the back got away, but the driver was detained by the police; I've just had the information from Scotland Yard. The driver talked. Listen, Number Seven. All of you down there must watch events very closely. Telephone me later . . . say twelve o'clock . . . with your report. Then I will be able to give you more information about the Buick.'

'Right,' said Quinion.

'Is there anything else?'

Quinion hesitated for a moment. It was difficult, talking over the telephone without being able to mention names, but he wanted to tell Craigie that Alleyn was the owner of the Café of Clouds; unless Number One of Department 'Z' already knew that, it might be of considerable importance.

'Yes,' he said finally. 'The invalid claims ownership of some of the clouds.'

Craigie hesitated in turn, working the queer statement out in his mind. As he answered, Quinion could almost see the corners of those grim lips twitching.

'I see what you mean.'

'Is it news?'

'Yes. Anything else?'

'Nothing,' answered Quinion.

'All right, Number Seven. Telephone at twelve, or as soon after as you can. . . .'

'Right.' Quinion put the receiver on its hook thoughtfully, then smiled as Smith entered the parlour, frowning impatiently.

'Are you coming?' demanded the Canadian. 'Or what?'

'Or what,' said Quinion. 'Sorry, Smithy, but if you will link up with men called Archie what can you expect?'

The Canadian shrugged his shoulders with a gesture of resignation. He had given up trying to understand any of the men whom he had met in his final effort to avenge himself on Thomas Loder. Yet he liked them. Now that Loder was dead, there was no real reason why he should continue to work with James Quinn and his eccentric friends, but it didn't occur to him to drop out.

He looked at the tumbler which Quinion had just emptied.

'I suppose that the hooch has made you sluggish, Quinn. Do you want me to put the car back in the garage?'

'Please,' said Quinion. 'But wait a minute. If you talk to me about "hooch" I'll sling the bottle at you. Use a civilized name and call it whisky. Meanwhile . . .' he paused for a moment, and the Canadian began to fill his pipe. 'Smithy, now that Loder is out of this business you haven't any real need to be in on this, have you?'

'I guess not.'

'It's a damned ugly business. If I'm not talking through my hat, there's a lot worse to come than has gone, and Loder was only one of the little men in the game. So if you feel like dropping out, drop.'

The man named Smith lit his pipe carefully. It was a characteristic of his to carry out all trivial movements with deliberate care, saying that it gave him time to think.

'Well, I suppose that's reason enough, Quinn.' He puffed at his pipe. 'But I don't know that I'm aching to get out. It's up to you.'

'I don't agree. If you stay in with us, it's a sticky end as likely as not. If it's up to anyone, it's you.'

There was a glint of pleasure in the Canadian's clear blue eyes. He leaned back in his chair, looking straight at Quinion.

'Well, if it's with me, I stay.'

Quinion stood up, banging Smith heavily on the back.

'Good man,' he said, smiling. 'Peter, I think we'd better have a spot to celebrate. Mr. Smith from Canada has joined us. . . .'

It was five minutes later that the three men were setting out from the Tavern to Cross Farm. It was dark, and they cut across the downs, where there was little likelihood of them being seen, and, in Quinion's opinion, no need for them to separate.

Quinion told them briefly of the happenings at Oak Cottage. He put no emphasis on the period during which he had been deaf, but the quiet conviction of his tone left no room for doubt. Neither of his companions needed anything further to convince them of the dead seriousness of the affair on which they were working.

They were still half a mile from Cross Farm when Quinion, sniffing the air, stopped in his tracks.

'Smell anything?' he demanded.

The others, stopping with him, were quiet for a moment. It was Smith who spoke first.

'Something burning,' he said. 'It's coming from the right.'

'The right?' Quinion frowned. 'I thought it was ahead of us. There's nothing to the right except . . .' he stopped speaking and broke into a run, beckoning the others. As they caught up with him he jerked out: 'There's a bit of a hill just up here; we can see better.'

Two minutes later he was standing still at the top of one of the sloping downs. To the left he could see a faint outline of Cross Farm, with two or three small glimmers of light winking across the darkness. To the right was Oak Cottage.

'There's nothing to the right,' he said quietly as the others came up, 'except Oak Cottage. And that won't be there for long. The place is burning like tinder.'

15

FUNNY FACE LEADS THE WAY

THE three men stood for several minutes watching the cottage burn furiously, and realizing that as it was swallowed up by the ravenous flames all chance of their learning its secrets disappeared. There was a grim smile on Quinion's face as he turned to the others.

'There goes a particularly dangerous little spot,' he said quietly. 'I'm glad I saw Reggie in that Buick; it would have been a nasty jolt if I'd imagined him tucked nicely in bed in one of the rooms of the cottage. However . . . ours not to reason why; ours to get on to Cross Farm.'

'I wish that there was a little more to go on in this business, Jimmy,' said de Lorne, after a few minutes' silence as they walked down the slope. 'Men wander about with guns, people drink whisky and go deaf, Reggie Chane gets kidnapped, Oak Cottage gets burned, Buicks get smashed up on the road through going at suicidal speeds, Thomas Loder gets shot, the Café of Clouds gets raided, a young and beautiful maiden walks about, I'm told, in fear of her life, and all, if I believe all I hear, because you, Jimmy, have butted in on a little game. Don't you think you could be a little more informative? I'll wager Smithy thinks more or less on the same lines.'

'There's much to be said for your reasoning,' Quinion said, 'but if I knew much about it I wouldn't tell you—yet. But I don't. All I know is that Loder was one of a particularly unpleasant gang of rogues, and he fancied that he was, more or less, king of the castle. Alleyn thought differently, and so did some of the others. Loder, you see, has been useful in working up a nice little connection of the primest rascals, but there his usefulness ended; he was put away.

'Working it out on those lines, I can see that, whoever they are, they're more than the usual clique of thieves and fences. Smith knows that they've interests outside England, and Smith also knows that the interests are mainly political. Putting two and two together, I suspect that we're up against something a lot bigger than you might think, Peter—but I don't *know.* That's what we're here for—to find out.'

'I wouldn't like to lay money on your power for telling the truth,' retorted de Lorne. 'However, don't let it worry you. I just thought——'

'Don't,' interrupted Quinion. 'You're wasting your time, Peter, and I hate to think that. Shh—sh——' He broke off suddenly, peering into the gloom towards Cross Farm, which was less than a hundred yards away. 'See that man?' he whispered.

De Lorne, following his friend's gaze, could vaguely make out the figure of a man approaching the farm from the direction of the main road. It was Smith, however, who whispered next.

'He's rolling, Quinn. He's drunk!'

The man was getting closer to them, and Quinion, patting the Canadian congratulatory on the back, saw that the man was reeling from side to side; as he came closer—he would have to pass them to reach the farm—they heard an unmistakable hiccup.

'Completely oiled,' murmured Quinion. 'And, by Jove, it's Funny Face. Let him get ten yards ahead, then follow him. . . .'

Between his hiccups and his continual efforts to control his legs, which refused to act normally, Funny Face was muttering to himself. As he passed them they heard him cursing volubly.

'Alleyn . . . whose 'e? Whose hanyone what's got the nerve . . . hic! steady, boy . . . hic . . . damn! . . . whose 'e? Whose telling me not to . . . drink? Hi . . . Hi woan stan' fer it . . .'

He reeled past, and Quinion stepped out of the shadows behind him, followed by de Lorne and Smith. Quinion realized that it might prove a heaven-sent opportunity for breaking into Cross Farm. He held the others back for a moment.

'If there's half a chance, de Lorne and I are going in. Smithy, you keep out here and watch for things to happen. If we're not out by half-past twelve, go back to the Tavern and telephone Victoria Nought.'

They walked swiftly to catch up with Funny Face, who was making still greater efforts to force his legs to meet Mother Earth. Peering ahead, Quinion saw the man's right hand dipping into his pocket. It was impossible to see what he brought out, but the Hon. James would have wagered that it was a key.

Funny Face walked round the front of Cross Farm towards the back of the large, rambling house. He was still cursing and muttering, and Quinion felt safe in getting within four or five yards of him. With de Lorne—Smith had stopped behind—Quinion followed their quarry into the small, unkempt garden which surrounded them, and were with him as he poked uncertainly at the keyhole.

'Now!' breathed Quinion. He reached out and for a second time in two days hit Funny Face heavily on the head with the butt of his revolver. The drunken man gasped and sank down inert. The key hit the stone slab of the porch with a metallic tinkle.

'Pick him up,' exhorted Quinion *sotto voce,* 'and carry him out to Smith.'

In less than a minute de Lorne had carried the unconscious man to the waiting Smith, and was back with Quinion. The latter inserted the key in the door carefully, and pushed it open gently.

The room into which they crept was in complete darkness, and Quinion was not disposed to use the torch which he always carried until he was more sure of the location of the other doors. Stepping forward with the silence of a cat, he found himself touching a large table. It was about four yards from the door, at which de Lorne was standing motionless, and Quinion, hazarding a guess that the table would be in the middle of the room, imagined that room was about eight yards across. Too large for a scullery, he decided, and yet not large enough for the living room of a farmhouse.

Still without a light, he sidled forward until he touched the wall opposite the door. It was strange that he did not hit against any kind of furniture, apart from the table.

Without a sound he made a complete circuit of the four walls. The one door which he found was in the corner of the room to the left of the door which led into the garden. Still puzzled, for he had not banged against anything at all on his round, he placed his back to the corner and switched on his torch. They were fairly safe from intrusion from inside the house now that the door was located.

The narrow beam of light stole slowly round the room. It was larger than he thought, and there were several chairs and another small table. He noticed that the table was covered with a white cloth, on which stood half a loaf of bread. It was impossible to make a thorough survey, of course, but on the whole it was in keeping with what he imagined—it was not a general living room, but one which was furnished with a semblance of comfort for the benefit of any stray caller. Quinion was fairly sure that Loder, during his tenancy, had not wanted it generally known that there were a dozen or more men living at Cross Farm.

De Lorne stepped softly towards his friend, who switched the torch out as the other reached his side.

'What now?' whispered de Lorne.

Quinion turned round.

'We're going further into the den,' he whispered. 'Have you left the other door open?'

'Ajar.'

'We'll leave this one like it too.'

He noticed that the hinges of the door did not squeak as it opened slowly, and he grimaced with satisfaction, which was increased when he saw that the room or passage ahead was in darkness. Apparently the occupants of Cross Farm did not live in the back quarters.

Listening carefully to make sure that no one was approaching, he switched his torch on for a second. The small, bright circle of light which appeared on the wall less than two yards ahead told him that they were in a passage. Sweeping the beam of light round, he saw that it ended a foot or two to the right; they would have to turn left.

The passage was a short one, and turned both right and left a few yards along. Quinion judged that if he went left he would find himself in the rear of the house again, and he was anxious to find the rooms which were likely to be inhabited. Consequently, he nudged de Lorne, and the two men crept stealthily towards the right.

There was another short passage, turning half right this time, and showing Quinion just that for which he had been looking. So far as he could see there were three doors leading from it, for cracks of light appeared on the floor beneath them.

Quinion gripped his friend's arm warningly.

'Keep close against the wall,' he whispered, 'and don't lose any time in getting past the doors. We should reach the main hall at the end of this passage—then we shall be able to find the stairs. We want a complete lay-out of this place in our minds, so that we shall know our way about.'

He stopped quickly, pressing himself close against the wall. From one of the doors there came the sound of a handle being turned. For a breathless second the two men waited, expecting every moment to be shown up in bright relief by the light from the opening door, but a murmur of voices, coming clearer as the door opened wider, relieved their minds.

'Fetch it later.' The voice was gruff and uneducated. The room was one of the living rooms for Loder's gang of thugs, thought Quinion. A second voice, clearer, and obviously that of the man who was opening the door, answered back.

'Why the hell don't you think first, Chevvers? You always were——' The sentence was chopped off short as the door closed. De Lorne heaved a husky sigh of relief.

'We're asking for it,' he whispered. 'Are you sure it's worth it?'

'I'm sure it might be,' Quinion answered. 'Don't be such a Jonah.'

They were creeping towards the end of the passage, and passed the two remaining doors without further disturbance. At the end, they found themselves faced with a closed door, from the bottom of which came a gleam of light.

'We've walked thirty-five yards,' muttered the Hon. James, 'and I'll swear that Cross Farm doesn't stretch any further. That leads into the main hall.'

'Going in?' queried de Lorne.

'Yes. Be ready to make a dash for the front door.'

As he had expected, the door opened easily to Quinion's touch. Opening it two or three inches, he looked into the room beyond. So far as he could see it was empty, although a large chandelier hung in the ceiling, spreading a bright light and showing the luxurious furnishing in all its glory.

'I win,' murmured the Hon. James. 'That's the front hall—and Thomas Loder spent a great deal of cash in fitting it out too. A couple of yards to the right there's a large settee standing a foot or so from the wall. It'll give us cover if we need it. Come on.'

It was touch and go whether they would reach the shelter of the settee before a door at the top of a flight of wide stairs opened more fully. Quinion saw it moving and crouched down, pulling de Lorne with him. They stayed there for several seconds, scarcely daring to breathe. Unsighted, they could hear the slow, deliberate footsteps of the man who was walking down the stairs. The very deliberation which the newcomer displayed convinced Quinion that neither he nor de Lorne had been seen. Easing his great body round, he was able to see the foot of the staircase and that part of the hall which led from the stairs to a massive front door. A heavy curtain, although helping to make their hiding place secure, obscured Quinion's line of vision.

He found himself clenching his teeth suddenly, and his hand, clutching the foot of the settee, tightened automatically as he saw the man for the first time.

A name, which he had first learned through Margaret Alleyn, flashed through his mind.

The Miser! . . .

Quinion remembered, foolishly, a stage portrayal of Shylock as he looked at the tall, spare frame of the man. He was clad in an ordinary suit of evening dress, but no clothes could have altered the parchment-like face, with its thousands of lines, some mere creases on the skin and others deep and scored, as though with a knife. A high, domed forehead was topped with straggling grey hair which seemed to have ignored the attention of brush and comb for years. The very incongruity of the man's hair in its disorder, and the immaculate perfection of his evening dress was startling. But that lined face, with its yellow skin looking for all the world like old parchment, compelled Quinion's gaze. The latter found himself staring, as though hypnotized, at two great eyes which were brown and yet gleamed almost red.

The Miser. . . .

16

THE MISER SPEAKS

QUINION shifted his gaze with an effort. There was something at once terrifying and yet fascinating about those glowing, reddish-brown eyes, which seemed to be gazing into his own. Relaxing a little to ease the strain on his arms, he found himself shivering; his shirt was sticking uncomfortably to his skin. It was not the first time since he had rescued the dog from Thomas Loder that he had experienced the unfamiliar sensation of fear which had overwhelmed him as he stared at the man whom he was sure was The Miser.

The old man was walking slowly across the hall, and Quinion, who had been able to see all the means of egress when he had made his first quick glance round, felt fairly certain that he was going towards the room which opened from the hall to the right of the settee. Easing himself round again he managed to see the slow, deliberate, and yet unwavering footsteps of the old man. It was from an awkward angle, for he could only look beneath the settee, but he saw the gleaming patent shoes stop, and heard the handle of a door turning. Then he could see the door opening inwards.

A confused murmur of voices reached his ears. It was obvious that the room into which The Miser was walking was not empty. Several chairs scraped, the murmuring increased, and then, as the heel of the old man's shoe passed out of Quinion's sight, a silence followed. The door closed before Quinion heard any further sound.

For several minutes the two men stayed behind the settee without speaking. Then de Lorne inquired, with a plaintive whisper, whether it wasn't possible for Jimmy to take most of his foot off his, de Lorne's, nose.

Removing his foot, Quinion worked himself into a sitting position, with his legs beneath the settee.

'Quite like home, isn't it?' he asked. 'Feeling comfortable?'

'I haven't been comfortable for five minutes on end since you dragged me out of the Café of Clouds,' de Lorne grumbled.

'Stop grousing or I'll put my foot on your nose again. Peter, did you see him?'

'I saw a pair of patent shoes,' admitted de Lorne grudgingly, 'but the rest of everything was hidden behind that size twelve foot of yours.'

'I only take elevens. Peter, unless I'm mistaken, those patent shoes clad the great feet of the Big Noise of Loder's little outfit. . . .'

'Seriously?'

'Of course I'm serious. What's worrying me is, how can we get into that room without being seen or heard?'

'Why not take a squint upstairs while the old devil's gone? It was an old man, wasn't it?'

'Very old,' said Quinion glibly. 'Twice as old as Methuselah.'

'You're lying again,' accused de Lorne. 'What I was about to say, is . . .'

'You mean "was",' interrupted Quinion pedantically. 'It's quite a sound idea. We might learn a lot from upstairs, but on the other hand, I'm mighty curious as to what's going on in that room. Listen. There's the front door, the door at the top of the stairs, two more along the passage up there and the one we've just come through, as well as the one through which our friend with the feet went so gaily. That means that we can be surprised and surrounded easily, but, with The Miser about . . .'

'The who?' demanded de Lorne.

'The Miser,' repeated Quinion firmly. 'I'll tell you all I know about him later on, but at the moment you'll have to be satisfied by thinking of that pair of patent shoes and call-ing their owner The Miser. As I was saying, while he's about I've a kind of idea that none of the lesser fry will walk into the hall. Don't ask me why; it's a pure and simple hunch, but I stand or fall by it. Now then. Sit tight in—or on—this settee, and play with your gun. You can keep an eye on all the doors and lead that easy life that you're hankering after at the same time.'

'What are you going to do?' demanded de Lorne.

'I'm going to glue my eye to that keyhole for a minute,' said Quinion with decision, 'and when I've got the lay of the land, I'm going to try to open the door an inch or two.'

'You're crazy!' opined de Lorne, standing up and stretching his legs. 'Take my tip, and leave well alone.'

'If you think this is "well",' returned the Hon. James, rubbing his arm gently to restore circulation, 'I wouldn't like you for a doctor. By the way, you *have* got a silencer on that gun of yours, haven't you?'

De Lorne nodded, offering Quinion his squat, ugly-looking automatic for inspection. Quinion glanced at it.

'Good. Don't worry about killing anyone. All the lads of this little shanty have asked for it more than once. And don't fall asleep on the couch, or I'll punch your nose.'

He grinned and stepped softly across the thinly carpeted hall towards the door through which The Miser had disappeared. Kneeling down, he looked through the keyhole.

Since first hearing of the affair in which Thomas Loder had been an active agent, the Hon. James Quinion had received many shocks. Nonetheless, the sight which now met his eyes made him draw in his breath in stupefaction.

He had a fairly clear view of the profile of the gaunt old man whom he thought to be The Miser, of whom Margaret Alleyn had spoken so fearfully and who had filled him, for a few seconds, with a fear akin to dread. The Miser was sitting at the head of a large table—Quinion could only see part of it—along the sides of which were arranged stiff-backed chairs occupied by men who were all dressed in the manner of The Miser himself: formal evening clothes. There was one big difference, however; each man, including the man at the head, wore a hat. . . .

Quinion, describing it afterwards, said that he didn't know whether to call it a hat, or a crown, or what. Actually it was more like a crown, a gruesome, grinning, spectre-like creation of a death's head.

'I could see seven of them,' he told Gordon Craigie later in the night. 'Seven seemingly sane and almost respectable citizens in evening dress, and all crowned with that damnable skeleton face . . . damn it, Gordon, it gave me the jim-jams! And I was just about to throw a faint when de Lorne tapped me on the shoulder.'

Quinion had, in fact, been oblivious of everything save the sight of those grinning heads and the mad gathering at the table. When de Lorne touched him lightly on the shoulder he spun round with a muttered imprecation. Seeing Peter, he grinned weakly.

'Sorry,' he whispered. 'I've just seen an improvement on Madame Tussaud's.'

'Forget it,' exhorted de Lorne urgently. 'One of the doors upstairs is wide open.'

Quinion glanced swiftly round the hall, and decided that a pair of heavy velvet curtains which hung over the front door afforded more comfortable and safer shelter than the settee. He motioned to it, and hid swiftly behind the curtains, leaving a crack through which he could see into the hall.

But for his sudden touch on de Lorne's arm, the latter would probably have given their presence away as two men walked from the room upstairs and began to make their way slowly downwards. They were carrying a trolley-tray laden with decanters and a dozen glasses. It was their dress, however, which nearly made de Lorne cry out, although after his brief sight inside the room downstairs, Quinion was prepared for anything.

Both men, obviously servants, were dressed from head to foot in a flowing robe on which was painted that same grinning death's head. Even Quinion, prepared though he was, shuddered. There was something horrible about the whole business, something . . . ghoulish.

Quinion, taking a chance, whispered urgently:

'Directly they reach the floor, step out and show them that gun of yours. Use it if necessary. Get towards the settee, so that they're both looking at you and away from me, and I'll get behind the blighters and clout 'em.'

He had scarcely finished talking than the two men reached the bottom step of the stairs. Directly the trolley-tray was safely deposited on the floor, de Lorne stepped from his hiding place. He was half way across the hall before either of the men saw him, and the threatening revolver choked back the cry that sprang to their lips.

'Stand away from the tray,' ordered de Lorne in a whisper.

The servants stood side by side, looking uncertainly at the man with the gun. They had no idea that anyone was behind them until one felt a blow on the back of his head and sank down with a grunt. The second was held in a grip of iron, and a vast hand was pressed over his mouth.

'Now, I'm going to ask you things and you're going to answer,' muttered Quinion. 'If you don't, or if you speak above a whisper, I'm going to drill a nice clean hole right through you. Get me?'

The man nodded, thoroughly scared. Quinion, satisfied that there was little likelihood of revolt whilst the fellow was faced with the threat of de Lorne's automatic, questioned quickly.

'Do you walk straight in there? Or do you knock first?'

'Knock,' whispered the other, staring into Quinion's compelling, flecked grey eyes.

'How many times?'

'Twice—with your knuckle.'

'Do you wait for an answer?'

'Yes. Spooks will say "enter".'

'Who will?' demanded Quinion, raising his brows.

'The old man . . . Spooks, we call him. . . .' The man was too cowed to grin, but Quinion found it hard to repress a chuckle. 'Spooks'. He would have to go a long way before finding a better nickname for the man called The Miser.

'Then you walk in?'

'Then I throws the door open and take a hold on the trolley and in we goes.'

'What then?'

'Then we goes up to Spooks and he says what he wants, brandy; I ain't never known him want anything but brandy, and we doles him a spot out.'

'How much?'

'He'll say how much.'

'And after that?'

'Then we goes all round, starting from Spooks's right, and pours out whatever they asks for.'

'And then you come out?'

'No. Spooks gives us a spot of his "shut-ear".'

'What the devil is "shut-ear"?'

The man was obviously regaining confidence. In spite of the figure of his companion stretched out on the floor in front of him, he felt that these two men threatened little harm. They were not of the type of Loder and Alleyn.

'Well, guv'nor, it's a dope what he's got hold of. He gives you a drop in a spot of whisky and you can't hear nothing. Then you stands by and serve out whatever they wants.'

'How can you, if you can't hear?' demanded Quinion. He was praying that the luck would hold and he would be able to carry out his plan before there were any further interruptions.

'They beckons with their fingers, and points. There's only brandy and whisky there.' He darted a look towards the two decanters on the trolley. 'I lay you can tell which is which, boss.'

'I'll lay I can,' answered Quinion. He looked across at de Lorne. 'Take those glad rags off that chap, Peter, and wrap 'em round you. Then cover this bloke. . . .' He looked at his informant with a grin.

'I hope you haven't been lying,' he said easily, 'because I would make it very painful for you afterwards. But for the time being I shall have to hit you over the head. But if I pass you a couple of fivers it'll be worth it, won't it?'

There was a gleam of cupidity in the smallish eyes.

'Blime, guv' . . . be a sport and give us a chance to get out of here. The Old Man's safe for a bit; Alleyn's away, and Loder's dead. We could do it now.'

Quinion frowned for a moment. Then he grinned, taking two five-pound notes from his pocket.

'I'll take you,' he said suddenly. 'Your pal's waking up. Is he in it too?'

'Give him half a chance, boss, and he'll fly away.'

Quinion dipped into his pocket again.

'Give him these, and let him run. Now, off with that cloak.'

It was madness, he assured himself three minutes later. Both the servants were by the front door, the one who had been knocked out blinking painfully in the light, and the other exhorting him profanely, but in stage whispers, to wake his ideas up. De Lorne, clad from head to foot in one of the cloaks, was bending down over one end of the trolley-tray, and Quinion was leaning over the other. With a grin he lifted the whisky decanter and swallowed a mouthful of neat spirit.

'Have a drink?' he suggested to de Lorne.

The other grimaced.

'Hope to the Lord it isn't doped with "shut-ear",' he said piously. 'All set.'

'Good. Now, here's to hoping!'

Yes, it was crazy. The Miser with a dozen of the men who were with him on some fabulous plan, was about to be 'raided' by two psuedo-servants, whose life would not be worth a moment's purchase if their identity was discovered.

Drawing himself up, Quinion rapped twice on the panels of the door. There was a wait of several seconds before the voice of 'Spooks' came to his ears. It was a firm, clear voice, mellowed with age. A gentleman's voice, and one which Quinion thought was somehow familiar.

'Enter,' said The Miser.

17

QUINION LEARNS MANY THINGS

QUINION was fully alive to the tremendous risk that he was running, together with de Lorne; but had the risk been twice as great he would have considered it well worth taking the chance.

He had no doubt but that Gordon Craigie had known of the meeting at Cross Farm, and the telephone call had been put through in order to make sure that someone was at hand. It was occasionally necessary for one of the agents of Department 'Z' to telephone the office, but only on the most important and urgent matters did Craigie telephone to an agent.

Quinion knew, too, of the small 'meetings' which were held sometimes at Oak Cottage; Margaret Alleyn had told him of them, and of The Miser . . . yet at the cottage The Miser had always been absent. Now, however, he was in attendance, and the meeting was a full one. It was the type of opportunity for which Quinion, in his more optimistic moments, prayed; nothing on earth would have made him hold back. The possibility of The Miser realizing at once that the two men who entered were strangers was the main danger.

Within two minutes Quinion was convinced that the first part of the gamble had come off. The Miser accepted him without question. He called, in that mellow voice which Quinion felt again to be familiar, for brandy, motioning when the small glass was half full. Hardly daring to lift his eyes, Quinion went round the large table, serving whisky or brandy to each of the men.

Apart from the grotesque appearance lent by the skulls which surmounted each head, the meeting might have been any ordinary business affair. Quinion could imagine any one of the men sitting at the board table of a dozen respectable firms in the city. Just such a meeting, he imagined, might be called in emergency at the house of any one of the directors at a time when all of them had dressed for dinner.

As he went round, pushing the little trolley, he was seething. Face after face appeared to him as familiar, and time after time he placed the men. One, a little Scotsman with a vast expanse of forehead and a few thin hairs spread carefully over an otherwise bald pate, was the managing director of Tunn, Son . . . Co., perhaps the biggest financiers in London. Another, obviously a foreigner, and sitting incongruously next to the Scotsman, had a tremendous beard into which he mumbled continuously. He was a man whose name struck fear into many a loyal Soviet heart. A third Quinion recognized as Brundt, the leader of the West German left-wing opposition, and a man of almost unlimited powers.

The conversation was stilted for the most part, but Quinion imagined that it was for the benefit of the servants. He found it difficult not to turn and look towards The Miser, but a display of curiosity was not likely to help him. He waited until the trolley was turned towards the man at the head of the table, then watched his man through his lashes.

No one could have questioned the great masterfulness of The Miser. In spite of that wrinkled, parchment-like skin with its myriads of wrinkles and the hunched shoulders which made The Miser's neck seem considerably shorter than it was, the strange amber eyes irradiated strength. The mind behind that high, domed forehead was vitally alert; Quinion imagined that the intellects of the dozen men in evening dress were dwarfed by that of their leader; yet every one of them was an authority on his particular subject. From what Quinion could judge, the strength of the meeting was half political and half financial, although there were four men whom he could not place, all of them foreigners.

Quinion had already primed de Lorne about how to try to frustrate their dose of 'shut-ear'. He watched The Miser carefully measure two small amounts of whisky into the two glasses which had been left over after the members of the meeting had been served. He saw the old man add deliberately a drop of liquid from a glass phial, and stepped forward to take the glasses. He breathed again when the leader of that strange gathering looked away from him, and tossed the contents of the glass into his mouth. Turning quickly, so as to hide de Lorne from as many pairs of eyes as possible, he emptied his mouth into a large handkerchief that he had held screwed up, in his hand. De Lorne with a quickness of hand that would have done credit to any magician, followed suit with his potion.

As Quinion turned round and replaced his glass on the tray, he saw the great amber eyes fixed on him penetratingly. Shivering inwardly, he felt the hair at the back of his neck rising.

Even at that moment he knew that he was afraid of the vast power of The Miser; if ever a man was evil, that man was.

For a few seconds that passed like hours Quinion wondered whether the trick had been discovered. The burning gaze of those terrible eyes, blazing in the parchment-like face that by itself might have been death, with the grinning image of a death's head on top of the high forehead, was as terrible as it was bizarre. A confusion of words hurtled through Quinion's mind as he averted his gaze, until three of them seemed to hammer against his forehead in a frenzy to escape.

The Death Miser!

He went cold suddenly. The Miser's great orbs turned away and the old man spoke quietly to a perfectly groomed, middle-aged Englishman sitting at his left hand. Quinion knew the other to be Julian Hatterson, the guiding hand behind a huge combine of super-markets which had branches in every town and village of any size in the United Kingdom.

Standing back from the table, and moving only when he was beckoned by one or other of the men, he examined the gathering more closely. Next to Hatterson sat Brundt, the German, and next to him Tunn, the Scottish financier. Two lesser lights in the financial world sat next to Kretterlin, the agent of the Soviet, who was placed beside Tunn. Then there were the four men whom Quinion did not know, but on The Mister's immediate left was Martin Asterling.

Asterling. Quinion tried to imagine a reason which could explain his presence at that mad meeting. He was a German who had taken on American nationality twenty years before and had made a world-wide name for himself in films. Recently he had been reported in the Press to be making an extensive tour of Europe in search of talent, and to study the possibilities for film production in England.

JOHN CREASEY

Still more inexplicable was the presence of the man who sat next to Asterling. Simon Hessley was perhaps the best known man in England. His interests were everywhere, and he had a finger in most governments, a word to say in most financial deals in the city, and a controlling hand in three great national daily newspapers. If England was ever forced to vote for a dictator, Hessley's immense following and tremendous popularity would practically assure his triumph; Quinion, his mind in a whirl, tried to imagine what benefit Hessley could hope to derive from what The Miser was planning.

Ten minutes or more had passed when The Miser tapped gently on the table with the small hammer which rested in front of him. Immediately the hum of talk ceased, and all eyes were directed towards the top of the table.

Quinion flashed a warning glance at de Lorne, who responded with a barely perceptible flicker of his eyelids. Hardly had Quinion looked away from his friend than the mellow voice of The Miser broke the silence.

'Brandy. . . .'

Quinion had to clench his teeth to prevent himself from laughing. A dozen of the greatest minds in the world were gathered round the table of this mummified picture of death, waiting on his words . . . and the word had been 'brandy!'

Neither Quinion nor de Lorne appeared to hear. It was obviously a trap; The Miser was testing the effects of his drug, and the slightest move on the part of either of the pseudo-servants would have meant discovery. But neither man moved.

There was a pause of perhaps thirty seconds before the leader of the gathering looked away from Quinion. The latter, uneasily aware of the power behind those flaming eyes, eased his neck a shade as he waited on the other's words.

The smooth voice, still irritatingly familiar to Quinion, went on in measured, deliberate tones.

'Gentlemen, we are able to talk freely now, and I am anxious to lose no more time. There is nothing to do beyond giving me your reports.'

The speaker broke off, staring malevolently at Kretterlin, whose deep, rumbling voice had interrupted him.

'Well?'

Even the Russian seemed cowed for a moment by the concentrated fury in that single world. He stuttered for a second into his vast, straggling beard, then threw his great head back challengingly. Quinion wondered at the man's perfect English as much as he admired the manner in which he faced The Miser. No. 7 of Department 'Z' was under no delusions as to the leader of that meeting. The Miser's expression was diabolical.

'There should be no servants,' said the Russian harshly. 'It is foolish. What you would call asking for it. . . .'

There was a hush which fell like a mantle over the whole room. No one there beyond the Russian dared have interrupted, and the others seemed to be waiting for the eruption which would ensue.

The Miser sat staring at the Russian for several seconds. There was no movement of any kind in his mummy-like features, but the great amber eyes flamed terribly, and his voice, when it broke the pregnant silence, had lost much of its smoothness; it was harsh and arrogant.

'Kretterlin, I will overlook your interruption this time. It is the first visit which you have made to a full meeting, although I have heard from Alleyn of your tendency towards . . . insubordination. Should you endeavour to advise me again I will arrange for your interest in our campaign to be terminated. You understand?'

The words cut like a knife into the silence, and several of the men seemed to shrink back. The Russian was no craven, however, although his leader's manner seemed to take away much of his confidence. It was replaced with a kind of desperate fury, the fury of a fanatic. The man moved from his seat suddenly, sending his chair backwards with a crash. His eyes, set deep in their sockets, blazed.

'By Saint Peter! I haff not been address like that since the day of the Purge. Those servants, they are dangerous! I, Kretterlin, say it! They must go!'

Quinion's face expressed nothing but a vague apprehension such as he considered likely in a man who could hear nothing but could see the anger of the Russian, and de Lorne might have been his twin. Yet both men were holding their breath in suspense. If Kretterlin got his way their efforts would have been fruitless . . . beyond the knowledge of many of the men behind The Miser's scheme; but it was knowledge of the scheme itself that Quinion wanted.

For a full minute there was a clash between the two great personalities. The Miser uttered no word; Kretterlin returned the burning glare of the amber eyes which gleamed almost red with a fury that nigh matched it. There was a tension like the calm before a whirlwind.

Like a knife, the tension was broken by Simon Hessley, and once again Quinion found himself hard put to it to stop from laughing. Hessley's voice—its timbre was familiar to the whole of England—broke in with a softness that seemed puny against the hard voices of The Miser and Kretterlin.

'Are we going to spend the rest of the evening like this? Kretterlin, you haven't been here before; those servants will be stone deaf for five or six hours. Miser'—the name seemed bizarre coming from those curling lips, but Hessley used it almost familiarly— 'Kretterlin is quite right, and perfectly justified in objecting; but he will submit if we assure him that we know the servants are safe.' He glanced for a moment towards the Russian, who had picked up his chair and was sitting in it calmly. 'Is that good enough, Kretterlin?'

'I suppose,' the Russian growled, eyeing The Miser sullenly. 'I only ask you to be reasonable.'

Quinion was amazed at the way in which The Miser accepted this. He lifted his hand as though admitting that he had been in the wrong. Yet the Hon. James wondered; it had been too easy—and there was an enmity existing between the Russian and his leader; of that the agent of Department 'Z' was sure.

The Miser continued as though there had been no interruption, however, and the Hon. James had to jerk his mind back quickly in order to follow the trend of the old man's words. The Miser's voice had regained its mellowness, making Quinion search his mind for the memory which would tell him where he had heard it before.

'I will have your reports in the order at which you are sitting, starting from my right. Asterling, please. . . .'

If Quinion had wondered at the film magnate's presence, he was aghast at his words. All over the world movie and television films of tremendous popular appeal had been made; but all had a militarist leaning; and they were carefully calculated to stir up enmity between countries. The fact seemed to hit Quinion between the eyes: it was incredible that these men, trusted leaders of the people, were actually propagating war. But that was what they were doing . . . *planning a World Revolution!*

Each man gave his report concisely but with complete confidence. Brundt, Kretterlin, and Simon Hessley spoke of political support which would be forthcoming from their respective countries. It made Quinion's head reel; war on a vaster scale than ever before was being planned for no other purpose than the enrichment of the members of The Miser's organization. The little Scotsman, Tunn, spoke in millions of pounds, reeling off figure after figure. He was obviously the financial genius of the campaign, and deposed a complete statement of the expenses incurred and the profits which should accrue. Nothing had been omitted, and Quinion was staggered as he heard the Scotsman talk calmly of market after market which was completely under the control of one or other agent of the vast scheme. War would enable prices to be forced up, bringing with them tremendous power to the members of the organization.

As each man spoke Quinion realized more fully the far-reaching effects of the scheme. Every Power in the world would have high officials corrupted by their association with the organization. In each Power one man would be at the head of the organization, and in turn would be directly responsible to the World Council, at the head of which was to be the man whom Quinion knew as The Miser. Two of the greater Powers were to be outside the war, thus enabling food supplies to be maintained, but supplied only through the Council. Outside of the two countries bitter hatred of one nation for another was to be carefully nursed into blazing flames. Hessley would be at the head of affairs in Great Britain, Brundt would control activities in Germany, and Kretterlin would hold sway over the Soviet. Men of world-wide fame were mentioned as leaders of the other great Powers.

And war was to be fanned into flame by a series of ghastly outrages in towns near the borders of European and Asiatic countries!

Quinion wondered whether he was going mad. Standing at one end of the trolley-tray, with de Lorne at the other, his face held a vacant expression which suggested that he was not only deaf, but half-witted. Beyond beckoning them from time to time and pointing to whichever decanter held the favourite spirit, none of the men who sat round the table appeared to notice the servants. The grinning skull which crowned each man's head, the mummy-like face of the man who sat at the head of the table, his great amber eyes turned only to the speakers as they took their turn, the tremendous powers which the organization controlled and the fearful campaign that it was staging, all seemed part of a terrible nightmare from which he would wake up in a sweat of terror. From time to time he eased his neck and swallowed hard.

Julian Hatterson had finished speaking of the food combines which would be controlled, and The Miser, still sitting motionless, seemed to be weighing his words. He spoke suddenly, with that mellow voice which could change in a moment from silkiness to arrogant harshness.

'Thank you, gentlemen. The plans have been perfectly conceived and admirably carried out. We have now but to wait for confirmation from countries which are not represented here to-night; then we can strike; and we shall strike according to the following instructions. . . .'

He paused for a moment, looking at each member of the company as though inviting comment. None came, and he went on slowly. Quinion, regarding him through half-closed eyes, thought madly that Death was speaking. For the words spelt death for millions of people!

'On the third of October every broadcasting station will be run by our agents. Notice will be given out recording the various outrages which have occurred in various parts of the world. Speeches will be made of an inflammatory nature calculated to stir the blood of all who listen, filling them with a lust for vengeance which can only be brought about through war. In some cases the broadcasting stations of one

country will transmit the speeches from another, until it
will be impossible for the ruling Governments to make any
other decision than settlement by war.'

The great amber eyes glowed with a fanatical light
against which the parchment-like skin seemed to take on an
even greater resemblance to death.

Death speaking!

The Miser went on:

'There will be such slaughter as never before—but only
by that slaughter can our ends be achieved. It will mean
death; death to millions; and death to the madness of World
Peace. That death I have been planning all my life; it is the
nature of man to fight, *and man shall fight!* We of the World
Council will control the destinies of all the nations, because
of the power which we shall hold.

'But remember—it will mean death. And to any who
may feel soft-hearted only death can come. We shall be ruth-
less. We must have power—which is wealth!'

The voice had lost its mellowness. It was harsh, cracked
with madness, broken with fury. One thin, emaciated hand
was raised and clenched.

'So will our plans materialize in the Death of Peace. I
have hoarded that death throughout my life, scheming,
planning, praying for it. Now it is at hand!'

The awful eyes glared feverishly at each member
of the Council, but before he spoke again there came
interruption.

Quinion heard the commotion outside the door before
any of the others had noticed it. He drew de Lorne's attention and the two men stood ready for action at the slightest
need. . . .

The Miser's hand crashed downwards—and at the same
moment the door burst open.

Arnold Alleyn stumbled into the room. One side of his face was lacerated fearfully, and the congealing blood against the whiteness of the rest of his skin had a ghastliness which seemed to freeze the members of the meeting; even the leader seemed aghast.

He spoke suddenly, harshly.

'What is it?'

Arnold Alleyn tried to speak, but could not. One trembling hand pointed towards Quinion and de Lorne.

18

QUINION GOES TO TOWN

APART from the two men themselves, Kretterlin was the first to realize the significance of that trembling hand. For a second time his chair crashed back to the floor, and for a second time his vast voice roared out. And it was to the diversion that he made that de Lorne and Quinion owed their escape. For the Russian, instead of aiming straight for the psuedo-servants, hurled his words at the tall, immobile figure of The Miser.

'I told you, you fool, I told you!'

The great beard jerked up and down and the deep-set eyes were blazing with fanatical fury, until a moment later a vast hand suddenly swept into the Russian's face and he was sent hurtling to the floor. Quinion, realizing that only seconds stood between him and escape, had leaned one hand on the table and vaulted over it. De Lorne did the same. Quinion's voice, quiet but imperative, broke the stunned silence.

'Your gun, Peter!'

He was at the door, glancing backwards towards The Miser and the other would-be rulers of the world. He saw a wicked-looking gun leap into Simon Hessley's hand, but before the latter had it under control Quinion had fired; Hessley dropped his automatic, cursing and shaking his right hand, from the fingers of which blood came coursing. Struggling madly to extricate himself from the chair on to which he had fallen, Kretterlin roared furiously in his native tongue, but apart from him and Hessley none of the others seemed able to move until Quinion and his companion were in the hall.

The fight was not over yet. Already there were three servants in the hall, and from the passage came the sound of running feet.

De Lorne sent the first man down with a right to the jaw, and the second, as he leapt towards Quinion, doubled up in anguish when the Hon. James let fly at his solar plexus with a straight left which had the force of a ramrod behind it. The third, catching sight of Julian Hatterson at the door of the room and seeing the automatic in the shop-king's hand, made a desperate attempt to guard the front door; he was short of average size, however, and Quinion, catching him bodily round the waist, heaved mightily and sent him sprawling towards Hatterson; the latter's bullet bit deeply into the servant's thigh.

De Lorne, meanwhile, had opened the front door, and with Quinion close on his heels tore out towards the main road, which lay some fifty yards ahead. Neither of them wasted time in looking round; if they were fired at from behind, the chances were against good marksmanship, for the clouds hid a harvest moon and it was almost impossible to see more than three or four yards ahead.

Neither men spoke. The urgent need was to get onto the main road and well on the way to Runsey village, and every atom of strength and gasp of breath was needed. Quinion cursed the dragging folds of the cloak which he still had round him, but it would have been suicidal to have stopped long enough to take it off; he gathered as much of it as he could under one arm and raced on.

His mind was working swiftly as he ran; one thing which worried him was the fact that Alleyn, having reached Cross Farm, must have had some means of transport. Had he secured a car, and was the driver waiting outside the grounds of the house? He was fairly sure that it was the case, and he realized that if the driver was one of Alleyn's men, and had heard the noise from the farm—already half-a-dozen shots had been fired and they were coming faster upon each other—he would provide a well-nigh insuperable obstacle.

He caught his breath as he saw the side lights of a car in front of him. It was standing in the road, and the driver was peering towards the farm. Quinion heard him talking to himself.

'Wot the ruddy blazes 'ave I 'it, now? Sounds like 'Ill Sixty an' a bit o' riot hact. . . .'

Quinion was less than five yards from the man, with de Lorne only a foot or two behind. The Cockney—still talking to himself, a form of Dutch courage which Quinion had often found useful—was crouching back against one of the large white concrete blocks which marked the end of the drive.

'Strike me if they ain't got a blinkin' Lewis!' The revolver fire was a regular fusilade, and was getting nearer every second, to the driver's obvious alarm. 'Hif it ain't a ruddy harmy, major! 'Ere, bilking or no bilking, I'm orf. . . .'

Quinion stopped, and holding de Lorne's arm, whispered breathlessly.

'Let him start up, Peter—then board him. . . .'

The words were hardly out of his mouth than the engine roared into action, and the driver let in his clutch fiercely, with an added jerk as a bullet hummed past his windscreen, and pressed hard on his accelerator. The engine roared protestingly but did its bit.

It was not until he had travelled a mile at something over forty miles an hour that the driver realized the presence of his passengers. Quinion, leaning out of the window at the peril of his life, for the bus was swaying from side to side and the hedge was dangerously close, indulged in a little gentle banter. He had only just recovered from the discovery that the 'car' was a not very sound taxi.

'Cabby,' he whispered, 'go as fast as you can but get us there safely. . . .'

The Cockney applied his brakes with that convulsive movement which is the birthright of every London cabdriver who isn't sure what to do.

'Gord!' he muttered. 'I've got hem wiv' me. . . .'

'Only some of them,' said Quinion cheerfully. 'Ease off those brakes, and move . . . oh, *curse* you! . . .'

The taxi was rattling along at a good fifty miles an hour before the Hon. James recovered from the shock which followed the driver's speedy compliance with instructions. Quinion's head had hit the woodwork of the window with a thud which made even de Lorne grin in sympathy.

'Hard luck, Jimmy. You seem to have scared the chap.'

'Scared him? I'll make him wish he'd never been taught the difference between the lighting switch and the steering wheel.'

'But for him,' interrupted de Lorne piously, 'and the Grace of God, we should be arguing with that Miser friend of yours and suffering something far worse than a bang on the head. Doesn't that look like the first cottage?' he broke off. 'Better tell him to stop.'

Ducking through the window the Hon. James advertised his reappearance by hooting the horn of the cab.

'See that pub along there?'

The cabby nodded without lifting his gaze from the road ahead.

'Then pull up outside, will you?' Quinion began to draw back into the dark regions of the cab when he caught sight of the driver's face as the man glanced round furtively. He eased himself through the window again.

'Percy,' he said affably, 'I think you and I are going to get along famously.'

The Cockney frowned, screwed his mouth in preparation for a complete and emphatic denial and then relaxed into a wide grin as he applied his brakes.

'Do yer? Now I wonder wot makes yer, guv'nor.'

The Hon. James opened the door of the cab as the vehicle slowed down, and jumped into the road, trotting alongside the cab until it reached a standstill.

'A perfectly sound question,' he announced grandly. 'You see, Percy, a couple of days ago we cooked breakfast together, and now we're going to try a spot of beer together.'

The cabby was climbing down from his seat, with his back to Quinion, muttering the while.

'You know,' he commented conversationally, 'between you an' me, boss, I been wonderin' where the blazes I'd 'eard yer before. What's yer gime, guv'nor? Larst time you was 'opping out hafter the poor cove conked out at the caff, and now ...'

Quinion placed his large hand over the driver's mouth.

'Things of that black nature can only be discussed after the ball. Come and have a drink.'

Half an hour later the taxi driver was reclining on the easiest chair in the bar parlour of the Tavern. He was enjoying himself as only men who are celebrating a rare holiday from wife and home can enjoy themselves. For the barmaid of the Tavern was comely if not beautiful, and it being after hours—de Lorne, being a resident, could be supplied with beer without fear of the law—she was able to devote her full attention to Percy. The driver had explained, between frequent tankards of dark brown ale, that after leaving Quinion on the previous morning he had stopped at a home from home in order to 'have one', overstayed his time and overworked his capacity, and had been compelled to lay up for a bit. Just as he was about to start for London he had been hired by Alleyn to go back to Cross Farm.

The cabby's one regret was that he had not made Alleyn pay first and ride after, but a neat piece of note passing on the part of Quinion comforted him; he accepted Quinion's instructions to be ready for a quick run to town philosophically.

Quinion and de Lorne went into the private parlour, and the Hon. James put through a call to Victoria Nought. He was speaking to Gordon Craigie within two minutes.

'You're twenty minutes early,' was Craigie's greeting. 'Anything much?'

'Bursting with news,' said Quinion. 'I shall have to come up to town.'

'*Have to?*' queried the chief of Department 'Z'.

'Yes, positively. Meanwhile, there's not enough down here to look after everything. There ought to be a small army, not two or three. What about it?'

The man at the other end hesitated for a few seconds. When he spoke his voice was even more deliberate than ever.

'Is it serious, Number Seven? Or just a precautionary measure? . . .'

Not for the first time Quinion confounded the necessity for speaking in riddles over the telephone. He was almost tempted to speak plainly, but the possibility of being over-heard was too great.

'I think it's desperate and vital. Get as many as you can over here and tell 'em to call at this place and ask for a man named Lorne.'

'All right.' Quinion could almost see the thin lips of the speaker puckering at the corners. 'I'll send them by road.'

'And you,' said Quinion, replacing the receiver and turning to de Lorne, 'are the man named Lorne. You'll have to forget the "de" for a bit; it'll do you good. Listen. Inside three hours you will have two large carloads of plainclothes men here. Take them to the farm and keep an eye open for anything and everybody. If you see anyone going out, don't stop them but follow them. Between now and the time they arrive you'd better wake the garage proprietor up and hire all the buses he's got that can do more than ten miles an hour. That's all . . . only keep an eye open for Smithy; I'm afraid the poor blighter has got mixed up in the meeting, but he might be under a lucky star too. All clear, Peter?'

'All clear,' confirmed de Lorne.

'Good,' said Quinion. 'Now I'm going to London . . . unless that driver is soused again.'

'Do you mean to tell me,' demanded de Lorne incredu-lously, 'that you're going to London in that cab? Jimmy, you must be growing grey. . . .'

The Hon. James leaned forward and slapped his friend on the back. He was feeling almost happy, now that the adventure at Cross Farm had ended in the discomfiture of The Miser and his band of budding dictators. There were

THE DEATH MISER

several things at the back of his mind which worried him, and others which puzzled, chief amongst the latter being the sudden appearance of Arnold Alleyn at the meeting, *without* his wheel-chair, and full primed with the fact of the changed identities of the servants. Of the former, his chief concern was for Reginald Chane and the man called Smith; but the triumph of the evening overweighed his fears for the two men.

'I'm going to town in that cab because I fancy no one will think I'm fool enough to do it. The Miser and his men are probably planning all kinds of messy ends for me, but it's a hundred to one against them thinking of keeping an eye open for the taxi. Got me?'

'Got you,' said de Lorne. 'Good hunting.'

19

NEWS FROM AUNT GLORIA

IT WAS nearly five o'clock when James Quinion, resplendent in evening dress which he had picked up from Runsey Hall on the way to London and changed into during the journey, reached the house near Whitehall. He dismissed the cabby, watched the taxi out of sight, and ascended the short flight of steps.

Gordon Craigie was dressed in pyjamas and a multicoloured dressing gown which, in its infancy, had made Quinion blink. He was sitting in the easy chair and smoking the drooping meerschaum; Quinion took his pipe from his pocket, incidentally removing an unsightly bulge in his coat, and calmly appropriated Craigie's tobacco.

The chief of Department 'Z' surveyed the vision of sartorial perfection grimly. He kept a watchful eye on his pouch, and stretched out his hand for it as Quinion absentmindedly slipped it into his own pocket.

'Sorry,' apologized Quinion. 'That tobacco's nearly as good as mine, Gordon.'

'Humph,' commented Craigie. 'You look as though you've been dining out. What's happened?'

'So many things,' said Quinion, 'that I'll probably fall asleep before I'm through. You wouldn't care to change chairs, would you? That one looks far more comfortable.' He grinned hopefully, but Craigie shook his head.

'Be thankful I don't make you stand to attention,' he said.

'You have sent the men down to Cross Farm, haven't you?'

'Thirty of them, yes.'

'Armed?'

'Revolvers and gas.'

'Who's in charge?' demanded Quinion, settling more comfortably into the swivel-chair.

'Number Two,' answered Craigie.

Quinion lifted his brows and puckered his lips. Number Two of the department was second only to Craigie himself, and rarely participated actively in the work on hand. Obviously the Powers That Be were fully aware of the desperate seriousness of the position; were, in fact, convinced of the necessity for prompt and thorough action.

Quinion had let his mind run on the problems during the journey from Sussex, but had found it impossible to cut and dry anything. The fact that he had been put on to the case, and that Department 'Z' was sparing no effort, assured him that much of the affair had been known to Craigie for some time, for Craigie was not a man to act on rumoured information. It meant, too, that incredible though the plans which he had heard put forward at the meeting of the World Council—he was already thinking of The Miser's organization in those terms—were, the preparations had actually been made; why else should Department 'Z' be throwing every effort into the frustration of them? Mad, fanatically mad, as that meeting had been, with the grotesque death's head crowning every man with a grinning portent of evil, it had been deadly serious. The Miser, with his high forehead, parchment-like skin, great amber eyes which flamed almost red at the slightest provocation, was not the leader of a fantastic band of perverted men who were aiming for something unobtainable, but was the leader of them, fantastic and perverted though they might be, aiming for an object which was already a definite possibility! The peace of every country in the world was being threatened. . . .

Quinion settled in the swivel-chair, eyeing his companion grimly. Gordon Craigie's hatchet-like face was immobile save for the movement of his thin lips as the meerschaum was lifted to and fro.

'Yes,' he said slowly, 'Number Two has gone down. I wouldn't have sent him yet but for your telephone call . . .' He broke off questioningly, as though demanding assurance that the call had been as imperative as Quinion had made out.

The Hon. James pursed his lips before speaking, and his flecked grey eyes took on a hardness which was rarely seen in them.

'I've left de Lorne down there, but someone more used to the game will be needed. I'll give you the whole yarn, Gordon——'

His quiet voice went on, rising a little and falling a little and always tense. He described graphically the whole of his adventures, together with Chane and de Lorne. The first raid on Oak Cottage, the apparent hopelessness of the position and the sudden, amazing turn of events. He did not place undue stress at first on the period during which he had been deaf, but his occasional references to it were more convincing than a dramatic description would have been.

Craigie sat motionless. Only twice—first when he heard of the burning of Oak Cottage, and secondly when Quinion told him of the arrival of Arnold Alleyn, did he display any emotion. On those two occasions the Hon. James could see from the way in which the meerschaum was held in the air for minutes on end that the chief of Department 'Z' had been surprised.

There was a silence which lasted for several minutes after Quinion had finished, and it was disturbed by a sudden yawn from the Hon. James. It took him completely by surprise, although he had been hard put to it to stifle a yawn several times during his recital. He grinned cheerfully at his friend.

'It seems that I'm tired, Gordon. . . .'

Gordon Craigie's lips puckered at the corners.

'Really?' he asked drily. 'Why, you've had at least five hours' sleep during the last three days!' He got up from his chair slowly. 'Take that collar off, Jimmy, and doze here for a bit. I've a number of things I want to do, but I want to talk with you before you go.'

Quinion affected a wideawake grin, but another yawn destroyed its effect. Without protest he unloosed his tie and sat in Craigie's chair. Within two minutes he was breathing regularly, dead to the world.

Gordon Craigie stood looking down at him for nearly five minutes before turning away with a smile on his lips. Tired! What a glutton for work Quinion was! Lucky, perhaps, but Department 'Z' owed a great deal to the Goddess of Fortune. Craigie lifted the swivel-chair back to its position at the desk.

He was still sitting in it, writing swiftly, when the harsh ringing of the telephone bell disturbed Quinion's slumbers. He opened his eyes, and watched his chief lift the receiver and speak quietly. He was talking for five minutes before he finished. Then he stepped across the room.

'Awake, Jimmy?'

Quinion yawned and stretched his great arms above his head.

'What news?'

'It'll keep for a few minutes,' said Craigie quietly. 'I want to talk about The Miser for a bit.'

'Carry on,' invited Quinion, reaching for his cigarettes. 'Anything about that laddie is well worth knowing.'

'Yes. . . . Very well worth knowing, especially his identity. That's your next job, old boy—discovering who The Miser is.' He paused for a moment, and Quinion regarded him idly. 'It's like this. I know a number of the men behind this scheme; I heard Hessley was in it somewhere three or four weeks ago, and that little curse, Tunn, and Kretterlin. I didn't know Brundt was in it, but I half suspected him, and I had no idea at all of Hatterson's connection, nor Asterling's. And I didn't know just how far the plans were prepared. Now that I do know, and we've got the date that they reckon to start the little game, I'm far happier. But I've been worried—very worried.

'It's September the twenty-third now, and that gives us ten days, providing they stick to October the third for the first move; as a matter of fact, they will probably make it earlier, now that they know some of their plans have been overheard —but three days is all we want to smash them— providing I can find who the leader is. This Miser has been haunting us for years. I've heard rumours of him, but have never been able to find anything certain. Once he is out of action the others will fade away; *but we must get The Miser.*

'I've just heard from Number Two. He raided Cross Farm at five o'clock this morning, first with gas and then with twenty men. All they found was the man who had been shot; every other man jack of them had got clear.'

He paused for a moment and Quinion broke in:

'Quick work, Gordon. The Miser may be old, but he's not slow.'

'It's quick all right, but it has points. They couldn't have cleared out like that if they hadn't somewhere else to go, and if they've gone to a definite place it will be easier to pick them up again. I've half a dozen possible rendezvous; you can have a cut at them all—providing you'll take the job on, Jimmy. . . .'

Craigie's thin lips were fixed in one straight line as he looked down at his friend. Quinion wondered for a second whether it was a leg-pull, but the other's seriousness was beyond question.

'Of course I'll take it on.'

The chief of Department 'Z' shook his head slowly and Quinion looked at him in amazement. What the deuce *was* biting Craigie?

'The last time you were here,' said the latter, 'you offered me your resignation. Because of the girl. I can't put you on this job unless you're prepared to let everything else go.'

'So that's the trouble, is it?' Quinion demanded. 'Well— Margaret's safe enough now with Aunt Gloria.'

He broke off, suddenly apprehensive. There was an expression in Craigie's eyes which he had never seen before; the chief of Department 'Z' seemed to have something which it was difficult to talk about. God! Surely nothing had gone wrong at Runsey Hall?

He went on slowly, eyeing his friend closely for the least sign that he had hit the target.

'I've fixed up with the two women to get across to France to-day. Colonel Cann is going with them.' He broke off again, his flecked grey eyes blazing. 'For God's sake, Gordon, what's happened?'

'I had a message from de Lorne when Number Two telephoned—a message for you.'

'Let's have it,' said Quinion. He wished Craigie would get it off his mind. Damn it, what had happened? 'Get it out. . . .'

'Steady,' repeated Craigie with maddening calm. 'It was actually from Lady Gloria Runsey—de Lorne called at the Hall in response to a telephone message to the Tavern—it seems that Lady Gloria is worried about Miss Alleyn. . . .'

Quinion's teeth snapped together suddenly. He had been afraid of that—only by telling himself unreasoningly that it could *not* be anything the matter with Gretta had he been able to evade bursting out with her name to Craigie. He could feel himself going white.

'Why?' The word was rapped out with the agony of his mind behind it. 'Go on, Gordon!'

'She went to bed before midnight,' said Craigie slowly, 'but when Lady Gloria went to see her just after one o'clock she was gone!'

20

QUINION MAKES A DECISION

QUINION felt stunned. Although the possibility of something happening to Margaret Alleyn had been at the back of his mind since the moment that he had left Runsey Hall, he had constantly refused to recognize the likelihood of it. Now that it had happened it was doubly a shock. He seemed unable to think, or speak. For a full minute there was such an expression in his eyes that made Craigie long to avert his gaze. Faced with personal calamity, Quinion's senses seemed to desert him completely, save the sense of hurt. His mind seemed clouded with an all-pervading darkness.

He broke through it suddenly with an effort that cost him more than anything else in his life.

'Just that?' he demanded. 'Nothing more?'

'Just that,' confirmed Craigie. 'The hall has been searched thoroughly, but there's no trace of her.'

Quinion kept silent for a full minute. Then he looked squarely at Craigie.

'Let me talk for ten minutes, will you?' he asked quietly. 'I want to straighten this out, if I can.'

'Carry on,' said Craigie.

Quinion weighed his words for a moment, while he sought automatically for his pipe. He took the pouch which Craigie passed, filled his pipe and lit it without realizing properly what he was doing. He wanted to straighten it out . . . if he could. No, not if he could; he was going to straighten it out; he *had* to.

As he started to speak, his words came jerkily and his sentences were spasmodic, but gradually he gained control of himself and spoke more naturally. Craigie uttered no word and made no sign throughout the whole time.

'I know that Alleyn is frightened of his daughter. She knows too much, and after to-night it was doubly dangerous. I fancy that he or The Miser realized that her knowledge and mine put together would have the whole plan at our mercy. I don't think there's much doubt about that. She knows something, although she may not know that she knows it— you get what I mean? —which, coupled with mine, would probably bust the whole show.

'Well—what is it? To-night I learned everything, practically, apart from the identity of The Miser. You tell me that is the most important thing left; well, we can take it that they think so too; so we can assume fairly safely that she could weigh in with the knowledge or a clue that would give us the knowledge. That's pretty sure. . . .'

He hesitated for a moment to light his pipe, which had gone out. Craigie was thankful, for the action said more than any words could have done; it meant that Quinion was getting back to normal.

'All right,' went on Quinion. 'The next thing is to find where she's gone. It's fairly safe to say that someone broke into the Hall and overpowered her. Say what you like, Gordon, but I *know* that she would not have gone willingly.

Alleyn or The Miser engineered it, but where did they take her? We don't know and there's the possibility that they murdered her straight away.' The words were so low that Craigie barely heard them; Quinion's face, which had regained some of its usual colour, blanched again. He took an obvious hold of himself, however, and went on more firmly: 'I don't think that's likely. It's more probable that they will think her useful as a hostage . . . and try to work her safety against my knowledge. Right. Then we're back at the question, where is she now?

'And it's there that I'm going to work on a hunch, crazy though it sounds. I'm going to work on the Café of Clouds. Alleyn owns it, and although he told Chane so, he probably isn't aware that Chane passed the knowledge on to me; Reggie would certainly say that he hadn't. The other thing is . . . the Queen of the Clouds. That gramophone record wasn't just chance, Gordon; somewhere in the business of The Miser and his World Council the Queen of the Clouds holds a mighty strong hand. I'm going to run that hunch . . . and if I'm not a long way out in my working, we'll get a line on The Miser through the Café.'

He stopped for a moment and looked questioningly at the chief of Department 'Z'; Craigie made no sign. Quinion went on, his voice hard:

'Nothing will stop me carrying it through, Gordon. If the Department doesn't think the idea worth running, I'll drop out and do it myself; but . . . the position now has developed into a battle between individuals. You have all the knowledge that you need to stop, or try to stop, the plans materializing, but until you have The Miser you can't be sure. The Miser realizes that too, and is working on the effect of having Margaret Alleyn to stop me from chasing him out. Of course, he knows that I can have passed everything on, but he also knows that there are some things that I can't explain . . . his voice, for instance, and the way his eyes change from amber to red; I would recognize them in a flash, but anyone working on second-hand knowledge would be less sure.

'Right. You'll grant me that I'm more likely to be able to find The Miser than anyone else in the Department. Let me carry on. I know that you're afraid that if I get any news of the girl I'll drop The Miser's trail and fasten on to hers . . . but you must see that before I can get her I shall have to get The Miser. It's a hundred to one on that—and it's worth a gamble, Gordon—isn't it?'

Gordon Craigie's eyes searched the flecked grey of Quinion's. He knew the truth of Quinion's statement that he was in a better position to search out The Miser than anyone else. It was certainly worth a gamble.

He sat on the arm of his chair, thinking out his words. Quinion eyed him anxiously. He knew that to work without the Department's support would be well-nigh impossible . . . and his mind was seething with the tremendous need for finding Gretta. Nothing must get between him and his object . . . only Craigie could hamper him.

'I'll give you forty-eight hours to work where you like,' said Craigie slowly. 'After that, if you haven't progressed, you'll have to drop out, or else work to my instructions. Is that good enough?'

Quinion nodded at once. The words of the chief of Department 'Z' gave him all the chance that he needed; for a moment he felt exhilarated, and his arm reached out to bang Craigie's stooping shoulders.

'Good enough? Why, I'll wheel The Miser to you in a bathchair inside twenty-four hours!'

Then he frowned. Something flashed across his mind—
the solution to one of the little problems that had puzzled
him for some time. The mental image that he had made
of the gaunt figure of The Miser being pushed along in a
wheel-chair had made him connect the leader of the World
Council with Arnold Alleyn.

'Damn me for a lunatic!' he burst out. 'Gordon, I knew
that I'd heard The Miser's voice before. . . . When Alleyn
forgot to be polite he sounded just like The Miser . . . Alleyn
and The Miser . . .' he stopped suddenly. For a moment he
had run away with the idea that the two men were one and
the same; but for Alleyn's bursting in on the meeting of the
Council he would have been sure of it; but both men had
been present at the same time.

Craigie's dry voice broke in on his thoughts.

'It doesn't work out, Jimmy. . . .'

But the Hon. James's mind had been working at top
speed. When he had seen Alleyn, or the man he had thought
to be Alleyn, in the Buick car he had caught only a glimpse
of him. When Alleyn had burst into the room at Cross Farm,
one side of his face had been terribly mutilated. He might
easily have been a man with a striking resemblance to Alleyn.

There was another point, too, even more convincing.
Alleyn was an invalid . . . almost unable to walk and usually
pushed about in a chair; The Miser's movements had been
those of a man who was infirm in body . . . Quinion remembered those slow, deliberate footsteps down the stairs. Against
this, the man who had burst in at Cross Farm had been in a
bad way, but he had been sound enough on his feet.

'It may not,' said Quinion suddenly, in answer to
Craigie's interruption, 'but on the other hand, it may be a
lot more likely than you think, Gordon. Listen. . . .'

He put his thoughts into words, and as he did so became even more convinced in his own mind that the man in the Buick and the wounded man who had betrayed his, Quinion's, identity at Cross Farm were one and the same . . . but not Arnold Alleyn. That crippled invalid and The Miser were identical.

Then he remembered suddenly that Alleyn's eyes were a queer, light grey. . . .

21

REGINALD CHANE REAPPEARS

THE notoriety which had fallen over the Café of Clouds had not affected the numbers of its clientele. In actual fact, it had had little effect on the quality, although a number of *the* people had avoided it after the shooting of Thomas Loder. It still remained, however, the most popular rendezvous for supper, dance and cabaret after the show, and London's stage celebrities were seldom missing.

Nothing had altered since Quinion's last visit, for although it was only three days since he had been there it seemed years, and the same illusion of sky and clouds had the same picturesqueness, and the same exquisite melodies from the same orchestra lulled the senses into a state of soporific listlessness which was aided by the heavy wines and the exoticism of the dances.

Quinion, sitting at the same table as before, cast his eye upon the numberless tinsel-pretty women, the occasional beauty, and the dozens of weak-chinned, vacant-eyed youths. He wondered idly whether he disliked those youths more than the ancients who vied with them for the privilege of escorting the women, and decided that he did; after all, the old men had probably aimed for something better at one time or other; the youths—Quinion steadfastly refused to call them men—seemed to have little more ambition than to sit, often tight in more ways than one, at the tables of places like the Café of Clouds and whisper insincere declamations of eternal love. A loathsome gathering, thought Quinion. He said as much.

'Agreed,' commented de Lorne without much enthusiasm. 'Y'know, Jimmy, I haven't a ghost of an idea why you've come back to this hole. It never was much to shout about, but now . . .'

'Now we've something more tasty to sample,' completed the Hon. James, 'it seems more than ever a waste of time. Quite true, Peter; it does seem so . . . but it isn't. There's much to do.'

He looked across the room towards the table at which Loder and Margaret Alleyn had sat on the night of the shooting. Three or four optimistic wenches caught his eyes and smiled at him through the haze of smoke. He grinned back automatically, and averted his eyes as quickly as he decently could. He cursed them mentally; they interrupted his train of thought, and he was trying to work out the secret of the shooting of Thomas Loder.

He was quite convinced that the man had been shot by someone either on the dais which held the orchestra, or behind it. The one other possibility lurked at the back of his mind, but he found it difficult to fit in. None the less it was with the latter theory that he played as he looked towards the small circle of white-painted flooring which opened outwards when the Queen of the Clouds appeared.

Had the Queen of the Clouds shot Thomas Loder?

Several times he had convinced himself that she had, only to reject the impression because he could find no real reason; for that matter, of course, there was no reason why anyone should have shot him, unless they had been instructed by The Miser.

What was the connection between The Miser, Arnold Alleyn and the Queen of the Clouds? Once he had discovered it Quinion was confident that he would discover, too, the identity of the former; but he was a long way from discovering it. For that matter he was a long way from finding anything which might put him in touch with The Miser, and thus Margaret Alleyn. And he had only thirty hours left with the support of Department 'Z'.

The time which had elapsed had not been wasted. He had payed a flying visit during the day to Runsey Hall, and talked for an hour with Lady Gloria and Colonel Cann. The latter, apparently susceptible to the charm of beauty, had called at the Hall, seen Margaret, and at once assured Lady Gloria that the young cub might have something in him after all. Moreover, he had offered to go with the two women to France, as Jimmy was so apprehensive of the consequences of Margaret Alleyn remaining in England.

Quinion had learned nothing more of the disappearance of the girl, however, although Lady Gloria confirmed his belief that she had, in some way which defied explanation at the moment, been taken out of the Hall by force.

Back in London, Quinion had had another, shorter talk with the chief of Department 'Z'. Without disclosing his actual plans, he had arranged to have at least two dozen men waiting for his call; they would be able to reach anywhere within ten miles of Whitehall inside half an hour. Then the Hon. James had worked out his plan of campaign, and as the dancer in the native costume of the South Sea Isles started the whirling flurry of her dance, he began to explain it, *sotto voce*, to the patient Peter de Lorne.

'Between you and me, Peter,' he said confidingly, 'I fancy this café could do with a couple of rockets plumped right on top of it; but not just yet; I want to have a look round behind the scenes.

'When the Queen comes out of that hole in the floor, I'm going to be at a table right near her; you see that empty one? I've reserved it under another name, and soon I'm going to collar it. The lights will go down soon, and the only one left will be the spotlight on the Queen.

'When she moves away from the hole in the floor, I'm going to slip behind her and let myself down. Yes, I know it's crazy'—he smiled as de Lorne let forth a gasp of incredulity — 'but I've been near that hole before; there's no one beneath that I can see, and it's open the whole time that our songster wanders round the room. There's crowds of time. You'll be sitting at the table, and if you don't see me back . . . I shall be able to haul myself up, if necessary . . . you can take it for granted that I'm having the time of my life; if there looks like being any fuss when I get down there, I'll pull a gun and let it go off; only if you hear a shot must you start any rescue work. Got me?'

'Got you,' announced de Lorne dazedly. 'I've got you for the biggest damned fool I've met in my life, and I've met some, Jimmy. Now look here . . .'

'Look here my hat!' interrupted Quinion. 'I've told you what I'm going to do, Peter. Now wait a minute.

'If I get down into that place and manage to dig out the information that I'm after without getting into the cart myself, I'll be at your flat by three o'clock. If I'm not there, telephone Victoria Nought, and tell whoever answers that Number Seven wants the Café of Clouds raided as quickly as possible, and raided thoroughly. The same applies if you hear a shot soon after I get down there; leave me to carry on until after you've arranged for the shanty to be raided. All clear?'

Peter de Lorne regarded his friend with an expression which conveyed the thought that he opined Quinion, his plans, his mind, his optimism, and his forbears little short of raving mad. He rested the tips of his fingers on Quinion's lean brown hand.

'You're bug-house!' he said firmly. 'For the love of Aunt Mary, drop it and try a new one, Jimmy. Why, you lunatic, it's thousands to one against you ever getting clear if the people here are in league with The Miser.'

Quinion pushed his nose into a tankard of beer.

'To all of which,' he said unkindly, 'once more, hat, Peter. You'd be surprised just how much a little drop of bluff dulls the brightest intellect . . . and I'm going to do some bluff. You see . . .' He leaned forward suddenly, and passed his fingers through de Lorne's immaculately groomed hair. 'You see, The Miser knows Mr. James Quinn, but he don't know the Hon. James Quinion.'

He was still grinning, howbeit vacantly, as though rapidly sinking from sobriety; the glazed expression in his eyes caused several observant damsels to nudge their partners, and they were rewarded when the Hon. James calmly added the contents of de Lorne's wineglass to his own tankard of beer and solemnly blew at the imaginary froth. Then he placed one unsteady hand on de Lorne's shoulder.

'You see, Peter, I'm drunk! You may not think so, but everybody else in the room who has looked this way during the past three minutes is convinced of it. And I want them to be convinced . . . especially the waiters. Because they'll tell the manager, and the manager will pass the glad news on, with the request that I be dealt with diplomatically, because I'm an important kind of cuss. Get the idea?'

'It's dawning gradually,' answered de Lorne, gently but firmly disengaging Quinion's fingers from his hair. 'But do you *have* to maul me about quite like this?'

Quinion nodded solemnly.

'Absolutely! Local colour, my hearty, local colour!' He tweaked de Lorne's nose, to the delight of a dozen onlookers, who were hugging themselves at the impromptu turn. 'Look at 'em, Peter; they're falling for it by the dozen. Listen. If the bloke named Quinn were to drop in he'd be in for a nasty time . . . but the bloke named Quinn is a down-at-heels kind of loafer. If the Hon. James Quinion, known to be drunk, is found wandering about beneath the hole in the floor, he'll just be led gently away . . . but he won't be socked. And if the thing comes off, I might be able to wander about down there and find a great number of useful things. It's a gamble.'

'A gamble!' declaimed de Lorne, ostentatiously moving a magnum of champagne from Quinion's reach. 'It's crazy, stark crazy. . . .'

Quinion shook his head belligerently. Two dozen watchers confounded the fact that the lights were going down and they would not be able to see the further antics of the social lion. To have seen them would have been well worth missing the Queen of the Clouds. But the movable section of the floor was already open, and the spotlight was directed towards the Queen's dazzling head-dress.

'I'm not crazy,' said the Hon. James with assurance. 'I'm just drunk, Peter! Now . . . the first thing, if there's any trouble, is to call up Victoria Nought. Keep it well in mind.'

Apart from that one beam of light which was playing on the exquisite beauty of the Queen of the Clouds, and the dimmed, diffused gleam from wall-lamps, the Café of Clouds was dark. The few people at nearby tables saw the

Hon. James rise unsteadily and stumble towards the empty table at which Thomas Loder had sat on the night of his death; then the Queen of the Clouds commenced to sing, in that silvery, flawless voice which brooked no denial; the insobriety of the Hon. James Quinion was forgotten.

The Queen began her stately parade round the Café of Clouds. All eyes followed her, the spotlight never left her; the rest of the room was in comparative darkness, and, more important still, was unobserved, save by Peter de Lorne. He saw the dim figure of Quinion step towards the opening, and watched his friend disappear. For several seconds he waited breathlessly, but no sound came. Minutes passed, and still the only sound in the room was the perfect singing of the Queen of the Clouds.

De Lorne made a mental exclamation of incredulity; Quinion had got away with it! Or it seemed as though he had.

The Hon. James himself was creeping across a brilliantly-lighted chamber which was completely bare of furniture, and empty of human beings. He had anticipated that all the underlings of the Café would be away from the under-ground room for at least half of the time during which the Queen was making her round—and his belief had been well-founded; the first part of the gamble had come off. But what lay ahead?

There was one door, and Quinion made for it without hesitation. His movements were cat-like in their soft-footed silence, in spite of the speed at which he moved. One hand was in his pocket, and it was holding the butt of a gas-pistol firmly. In another pocket he had a serviceable automatic for more serious purposes, but in view of the need for silence during the first part of his investigation, at least, he had decided to carry an ammonia spray, although he hoped devoutly that he would not have to use it. Even a drunken Honourable would not be easily forgiven the habit of dosing unfortunates with ammonia gas.

Quinion passed through the door into a narrow passage, also brilliantly lit, and which gave him the choice of two exits. Opening one door he saw that it was the Queen's dressing-room; he closed it gently and made for the other.

It led into a fairly large room which was furnished like an office, although Quinion saw no telephone. Again he had a choice of exits, and had decided to use a door which opened opposite the one through which he had come, when a sound of hurrying footsteps caused him to change his mind rapidly. He breathed with relief when the handle turned beneath his fingers. Opening it wide he stepped inside the room beyond, and blinked for a moment in the complete darkness.

He stood poised at the door, straining his ears to catch the direction of the footsteps in the other room. The man— Quinion could tell from the strides that it was a man— seemed to stop in the middle of the room and the Hon. James heard a drawer being pulled out; again he breathed with relief; in all likelihood the newcomer would not be coming into the room in which he was hiding.

Keeping the beam of light from the door and at a level with his waist in order to make sure that no tell-tale gleam could be seen from outside, he played his torch round the small room in which he found himself. It was practically empty of furniture, although a rough shelf plugged into the wall, and a chair next to a small table, suggested that it was used occasionally. The walls were distempered a sickly green, and so far as he could see there were no pictures.

He switched the light off, and waited for further sounds outside. Once more the drawer was moved, and the sliding sound ended this time with a click which suggested that it had been pushed home. The man hesitated at the table, then walked away. Quinion heard his footsteps gradually getting fainter.

Quinion had decided that it was safe to move from the room. He had ascertained that there were no other doors than the one through which he had entered . . . when a movement behind him made him swing round. For a moment he had been afraid of an attack, but he could see nothing, although his eyes were accustomed to the blackness. He waited, then was about to move again, when the sound was repeated. He told himself that it had seemed more like a groan than anything else, then decided that his nerves were playing him tricks; but a second repetition gave no room for doubt. There was someone in the room—and that someone was moaning!

With his back towards the door he played the light from his torch on the ground. Huddled in one corner was the figure of a man. . . .

Quinion cursed inwardly. The prisoner—tightly bound cords round the man's ankles and wrists allowed no question of his being captive—was trying to move, and with every twist of his body he groaned, drawing in his breath with a short, agonized gasp. Quinion looked at the face, cursing again as he saw the ugly, gaping wound in the man's forehead, and the congealing blood which had coursed down his face and made it practically unrecognizable.

Quinion would have recognized the captive, however, even had he not known him from the neat grey suit and the Old Addusion tie.

It was Reginald Chane!

22

'His Eyes Turned Red!'

A DRINK of neat whisky from the flask which Quinion always carried with him worked wonders with Chane, and when Quinion had cleansed his friend's face as well as he could with a dry handkerchief, Chane, although looking like a man bordering between life and death, actually felt comparatively fit.

'Feel like talking?' asked Quinion. 'There's a lot I'd like to know.'

'Give me time,' said Chane. 'And forgive me if I gabble a bit; I've a hell of a lot I'd like to tell.'

He took another mouthful of whisky, settled himself on the only chair in the room, and began to talk.

'There isn't a great deal the matter with me,' he began. 'When I was hiked out of Oak Cottage, Jimmy—a clever bit of work that, by the way; the whole of one wall in that big room slides along——'

'It doesn't,' broke in Quinion. 'The whole damned shanty has been fired.'

'And a good thing too,' said Chane. 'Oak Cottage is—or was—one large hell of a place. Anyhow, after they dragged me out of the room they gave me the needle, and I felt nasty for a bit after waking up. I was here then, by the way, and they treated me more or less decently until I had a difference of opinion with the dear Mr. Alleyn and socked him one. His bodyguard socked back, and since then—twenty-four hours ago, I reckon—I've been tied up here like two russed chickens.'

'About Alleyn,' interrupted Quinion. 'Is he an invalid? Or can he walk?'

'He can walk. In fact, he can't be more than forty-five, actually.'

'Carry on,' said Quinion.

'You know now just about all that happened to me—but I heard the deuce of a lot before the argument with Alleyn. You see, I got tired of sitting in here and playing patience, so I tried a bit of lock-picking which came off, and wandered round for a bit. I anchored in a little room across the passage . . . it seemed like any ordinary actresses' dressing-room, to tell the truth, Jimmy. . . .'

'It is,' interrupted Quinion again. 'The Queen of the Clouds uses it.'

Chane whistled beneath his breath.

'Jove! So we're at the Café, are we, James? Who'd have thought it. But to continue.

'I'd just got in when someone came along the passage, and I ducked beneath a dressing-table which had casement round it—a perfect hiding-place, James. Then Alleyn came in—I recognized his voice—and another fellow whom I couldn't place; I daren't look out, of course. They pottered about for ten minutes without saying much, and I gathered from the few words that did drop out that they were making-up.'

'Didn't they say anything that might have been useful?' queried Quinion hopefully.

'Not that I knew.' Chane rubbed his nose and squinted at his finger in the gloom. 'No—not that I knew,' he repeated. 'Wait a minute, though. They had a little difference about a date; Alleyn maintained that "it"—the Lord knows what "it" was—couldn't be brought forward so much, and the other man said that it not only could, but would be. Alleyn gave in without putting up a decent show. . . .' He broke off suddenly. 'As a matter of fact, Jimmy,' he put in, 'I couldn't swear that it was Alleyn who protested; the voices were devilish alike sometimes.'

'Hum,' commented Quinion. He paid less heed to the similarity than he would have done had he not been driving a theory through his mind. A theory which covered the identity of The Miser. 'This "it", Reggie; can you remember how it was brought in?'

Chane was silent for a few seconds before he went on slowly:

'Ye—es. . . . The old date was the third of October, and the new one the twenty-fifth of September. One of them asked whether it was wise to make it so quickly, and the other said definitely "yes". They only mentioned it in passing, Jimmy.'

Quinion's mind was working rapidly. There could be only one thing to which 'it' referred; that was the date on which The Miser intended to stupefy the world with his dastardly plot, bringing the nations to war; and it had been brought forward eight days! It was already past midnight, and the day was the twenty-fifth of September. *The day.* . . .

There was no time to tell Chane of the events which had led up to his, Quinion's, presence at the Café, and he made no comment. Chane went on:

'They had started to go, and you can take it from me, James, that I was glad of it. That dressing-table was at least three sizes too small, and my legs were aching like the deuce. I saw the light go out, heard them going along the passage, and after giving them a couple of minutes, crawled out myself; and I hadn't stretched my legs before Alleyn came back.

'I hadn't an earthly. The blighter must have had an idea that all was not well, and he made no sound as he flung open the door and switched the light on. He stared at me with those queer eyes——'

"So," he said, "you are not tired of investigating yet, Mr. Chane?"

'You'll grant me, Jimmy, that the circumstances were a bit trying. I said a dirty word or two and chivvied him a bit . . .'

Chane stopped, as though re-living the moment of which he spoke, and Quinion, used to the ways of his friend, waited expectantly on his next words. Had he been able to see the other man he would have been astonished at Chane's expression, which mingled horror with sheer incredulity.

'And then, Jimmy, believe it or not, *his eyes turned red!* I saw them changing gradually—they're a steel kind of blue-grey, ordinarily—they seemed to go white, then yellow, then red! . . .'

Chane broke off, and Quinion felt a surge of triumph run through his mind. He had not been wrong! Alleyn and The Miser were actually one and the same. He had no thought to question Chane's statement, but allowed his mind to run on his discovery. Alleyn was The Miser!

Chane went on slowly.

'There you have the whole of it, Jimmy. I couldn't resist having a go at Alleyn, but a couple of cavemen rolled up to his support and I had the worst of it.' He leaned back in the chair for a moment, took another mouthful of neat whisky, and sighed. 'I wish I could slip between the blankets.'

Quinion seemed not to have heard him. The new turn of events was of colossal importance, and he could see no certain way in which to prevent The Miser from carrying out his threat of dropping his bomb on the edifice of World Peace. Chane, although fit enough to talk, would not be able to tackle much in the way of opposition; and Quinion was between two stools. It was imperative to inform Gordon Craigie of the significance of September the twenty-fifth; and it was equally imperative to keep on the trail of The Miser in order to stop, or stand a reasonable chance of stopping, that bizarre would-be Ruler of a World Council from acting before the chief of Department 'Z' could move.

On top of which there was the safety of Margaret Alleyn.

He had striven to put all thought of the girl behind him, but it was impossible. Now that there was to be no waiting period his theory that she would be safe as a hostage was exploded. He was convinced that she was in extreme danger—and there was nothing at all that he could do to ensure her escape from The Miser and his satellites.

He had been with Chane for about twenty minutes, which meant that it was half an hour since he had first disappeared into the hole in the floor. The Queen of the Clouds, even in her most generous moods, rarely appeared in the Café for more than thirty-five minutes, for the last ten of which she was usually standing near the spot from which she had first emerged. There was just the chance that he would be able to get back, but it was a thin one.

Chane was standing up, moving his knees up and down gingerly. He had been massaging his arms and legs throughout the length of his story.

'How does it go?' queried Quinion anxiously.

'I couldn't walk a mile,' returned Chane. Unable to see his friend because of the darkness, he sensed the other's anxiety for instant action, and realized something of the urgency of the situation. He gripped Quinion's shoulder suddenly.

'Look here, Jimmy; I'm all right. Carry on as if I was outside this damned hole instead of inside it.'

Quinion gave the ghost of a chuckle.

'Don't be a ruddy fool,' he said briefly. 'Take this gun—it's ammonia, not lead—and follow me. Use it if you see anyone; or rather, if anyone gets close enough; the range is three feet. There might just be a chance of getting word to de Lorne. . . .'

The larger room was still ablaze with light, and the passages equally flooded. Quinion, listening for a second outside the dressing-room of the Queen of the Clouds, satisfied himself that she was not there; a moment later he heard that flawless voice raised.

'She's still at it,' he murmured. 'If only we can get through. . . .'

There was the sound of raised voices from behind them, followed by the lower tones of Mr. Arnold Alleyn. Footsteps echoed along the passage, and Alleyn's voice, soft and purring but distinct, came threateningly. Only the bend in the passage saved them from being seen.

'Shoot anything on sight,' said Alleyn.

Directly ahead of the two men was the door which led to the small chamber beneath the hole in the floor. Quinion pushed Chane inside and closed it.

'Now hoist yourself on my shoulder, and when you get on top, dash over to de Lorne. He's at the same table as we were the other evening. Tell him to get through to Victoria Nought for the raid on the Café, and to mention specially that the date is not the third, but the twenty-fifth of September. Ready. . . .'

The sound of voices came clearly from the other side of the door. The men whom Alleyn had sent to look for Chane—there was little doubt but that Chane's disappearance had been discovered—were obviously nonplussed by the closed door, and Quinion imagined that they were afraid to break in on the Queen of the Clouds. It was a question of seconds only.

Chane, his right foot on Quinion's linked hands, tried to hoist himself up, but stumbled. Quinion gasped, and Chane gritted his teeth for another effort. Then, without warning, the floor of the chamber in which they stood began to rise!

Quinion released his hands and looked upwards. He knew what was happening, realizing that from the point of view of his own safety it was providential. The floor of the chamber was operated by electricity, and moved upwards and downwards to enable the Queen of the Clouds to make her dramatic entry into the Café. Both he and Chane would be able to get out—but there was no possible chance of his getting back—and The Miser, knowing that Chane had escaped, would lose no time in putting his plans into operation.

He was working the situation out as the moving floor carried the two men upwards to safety. It would be at least half an hour before the Café of Clouds could be raided. In that time the plans which The Miser had could be acted upon. Instructions could be sent to every big country in the world, and the revolution which the World Council had engineered would have commenced on its work of destruction. . . .

Quinion had little doubt of its ultimate failure, but he knew that it would be a tremendous shock to the existing order of things, and a shock from which it would take years for the world to recover. He could see in his mind's eye the chaos into which the civilized nations would be plunged. Lawlessness would become rife, looting and pillaging would make a mad whirlpool of the baser nature of man, and the nations would be fighting for their very lives, destroying the civilization which they had helped to build.

Quinion's mind was in a whirl. If the Café could be raided at that moment, the whole colossal scheme could be wrecked, and the truth could be broadcast in order to counteract any efforts that the World Council did make afterwards. But in half an hour the ball would have commenced its fearful roll downhill.

His head was on a level with the floor, and he could see hundreds of feet tapping the floor in order to swell the roar of applause for the Queen of the Clouds. Gradually he saw more of the Café; then his vision was obscured by a shimmering gown of white covered with diamante. The Queen was making her last bow to that crowd of aimless pleasure seekers.

The heads and shoulders of the two men were above the floor, and a sudden shriek from one side of the room told Quinion that they had been seen. A moment later he vaulted upwards.

For the second time within three days, the Café was in tumult. The sight of Reginald Chane's face, with that ugly gash across his forehead and the blood, cleared from his eyes and mouth but still thickly congealed about his cheeks and hair, had caused panic. Women screamed and fainted. A man cursed, a table crashed to the floor and a dozen wineglasses dropped from nerveless fingers and splintered. Someone raised a cry of police, and it was echoed and re-echoed. Peter de Lorne was running wildly towards the hole in the floor.

JOHN CREASEY

The Queen of the Clouds was staring unbelievingly into the eyes of the Hon. James Quinion.

He heard the din about him and yet failed to understand it. He heard de Lorne's voice calling him, but continued to gaze, heedlessly, into the face of the Queen of the Clouds.

Into the face of Margaret Alleyn!

23

THE HOARD OF DEATH

QUINION stared thunderstruck into those glowing hazel eyes. He saw the sudden expression of incredulity which sprang into them and the wave of relief which swept across her face, replaced almost instantly by a fear ten times greater than any that he had seen in her before. Margaret Alleyn was terribly afraid.

His own mind was in turmoil. The tumult in the Café was forgotten in the urgent need of knowing why the girl was here, dressed in all the regalia of the Queen of the Clouds, singing so beautifully. It was mad—mad! The other night when Margaret Alleyn had been sitting with Loder, the Queen had appeared—a great hope sprang into his mind, only to be lost as quickly as it had been found. The thought that there might have been some coincidence of amazing likeness disappeared as he realized that she had recognized him. What was she doing here? Did it mean that her disappearance from Runsey Hall had been of her own free will? Was it possible that she had been an agent of The Miser from the beginning, hoaxing him, Quinion, by her beauty and her unspoken appeal to the romantic in him?

Was she—a spy—working against the powers of civilization, striving for riches which would be paid for in blood and slaughter?

Those questions and a dozen others rushed through his mind in the space of a few seconds. He stood there, looking at her. About him confusion reigned, tables and glasses were smashing to the floor, women were screaming and men shouting; a few stouter spirits were trying to restore a semblance of order, forming a small cordon round the Queen of the Clouds and the three men who obviously knew more about the Café than any others there.

De Lorne, almost at Quinion's side, had felt his arm gripped suddenly and swung round. Chane, his face white beneath the horrible reddish brown of dried blood, spoke urgently.

'For God's sake let's get out of here and call for help. Leave Jimmy to it.'

De Lorne frowned and hesitated for a moment.

'But——'

Chane had given way beneath the strain from which he had been suffering since he had been taken from the front room of Oak Cottage. He swayed on his feet, and would have fallen but for the supporting arms of one of the cordon which surrounded the hole in the floor. The man was a sturdily-built youngster of considerable strength and a remarkable lack of curiosity. De Lorne recognized him vaguely, but could not remember his name, which he learned, afterwards, was Felton.

'It's de Lorne, isn't it?' asked the latter, raising an eyebrow questioningly. 'And this looks like Reggie Chane. What to do with him?'

De Lorne glanced towards Quinion, but the other man was too engrossed with his discovery; it was his pigeon, thought de Lorne philosophically; with Jimmy goggle-eyed and Chane knocked out it was up to him.

'Get him outside,' he said, 'and take him to my flat—17a Gowert Mansions——'

'I know it,' said Felton.

'Good. Park him there—you'll find a man about—and forget this do until I look you up, or you can tackle me in a day or two. All right?'

'Good enough,' Felton assured him.

'Chin-chin,' said de Lorne. It was the devil of a job, of course, leaving Chane like that, but the crying need of the moment was to get out of the Café and telephone Victoria Nought. Quinion would have to look after himself. . . .

Five minutes later Peter de Lorne was hurrying towards a telephone kiosk that he knew to be at the corner of the road. He did not know, until someone brought a piece of lead piping down on his head with a sickening thud, that he had been followed—and a casual wayfarer, seeing him supported between two men in evening dress, told himself that yet another gilded youth had suffered from the effects of too much liquid refreshment.

The conversation between de Lorne and the man named Felton had not taken a minute, and at the moment when the former had begun to push his way out of the crush, Quinion had recovered from the physical paralysis which the sight of Margaret Alleyn had caused. His muscles seemed to become weak and for the first time he started to speak.

'Gretta——'

He stopped when a fresh outburst of shrieking came from the dozens of women who were still imprisoned in the Café. Men who had hitherto kept control over themselves cursed.

Someone had switched off every light in the room!

The sudden change from light to darkness brought the Hon. James to his senses. Swinging round he saw that no one was near him apart from Gretta—or the Queen of the Clouds—and he grunted with satisfaction. That meant that de Lorne and Chane had got away. He could safely leave the sending of a message to Gordon Craigie to them. For his part, if humanly possible, he had to get down into the rooms below the Café. No matter how speedily Craigie acted, he might yet be too late to avert the first catastrophe—for Quinion had little doubt that The Miser, seeing the hairsbreadth between success and failure, would begin his vile scheme by operating in those countries in which he knew his agents were in control, without waiting until he could stir up strife throughout the world. The flame of war would spread. . . .

Quinion had been too much impressed by the intellectual powers behind the World Council to doubt the perfection of its organization. If The Miser was confident of being able to put his plans into operation several days before the original date chosen for the broadcasting of his fantastic manifestos it was certain that every minor detail of the arrangements was complete, awaiting only word from the leader. Quinion, who had spent years following the trail of men whose plans, incredible though they were, aimed at the establishment of new powers, was not sceptical of the plans of the World Council. If the scheme was once started it would be impossible to hold it back. Already in the grip of industrial unrest and economic depression, the great countries of the world would find it impossible to maintain peace. Even if the plans of The Miser to gain complete control of food and materials were frustrated, the toll of life would be enormous and the damage to civilization greater by far than that which had followed on Hitler's equally fantastic scheme to control the world.

Quinion hardly recognized his voice as he spoke briefly to the Queen of the Clouds.

'How do you get down?' he demanded urgently.

In the darkness he could not see the expression in her eyes, but he could still imagine that terrible fear.

'But . . . Jimmy . . .'

One light hand rested for a moment on his arm, but a sudden movement of his whole body at the contact made her withdraw it.

'We haven't time for that,' he said roughly. 'I've got to get down . . . quickly!'

Without a word she stepped a yard or two towards the automatic lift. Equally silent, Quinion went to her side and saw her small, exquisitely shaped foot press a small circle in the floor; simultaneously they began to sink downwards.

The manner in which she had reacted to his action filled him with compunction; but he had been right when he had said that there was no time. Explanations of any kind would have to be kept until Quinion had made his effort. By exerting every atom of strength that he possessed, he put aside all thought of the woman at his side as Margaret Alleyn. As the Queen of the Clouds she could give him information that might prove invaluable—and every second counted. He gripped her arm suddenly.

'There's not a moment to spare. It's not a question of you and I—it's a question of thousands of lives which will be lost if The Miser gets away with it. Now—do you know what part of the place is his?'

The grim determination in his voice brooked no denial. She answered him quickly; yet had Quinion been able to see the expression in her eyes he would have wondered at it.

'Yes. Keep to the passage, without turning into any side doors. The first door that you see ahead of you is his.'

Afterwards Quinion wondered at his unquestioning acceptance of her information. At the moment he doubted her genuineness and treated her as an ally of The Miser, yet it did not cross his mind to doubt the truth of what she told him. His mind was full of the possibilities of the next quarter of an hour. He knew that the numerical strength of The Miser's forces was in the neighbourhood of twenty-five armed men, without reckoning the actual members of the Council; and as he thought of the odds against him he grinned ironically. From the outset it was as near hopeless as anything could be—but——

Somehow he *had* to prevent The Miser from acting until Department 'Z' surrounded the Café and brought the odds more even.

The lift had stopped and the Queen of the Clouds stepped into the passage. A dim light came from two wall-lamps, and Quinion was able to see the passage stretching out ahead of him. Walking quickly, they reached the door of the dressing room. Grim-faced, Quinion eyed his companion, but the softness of those hazel eyes, which looked at him with an appeal that no man could have resisted, softened his expression. Once more his fingers closed round the soft flesh of her arm.

'I'm sorry,' he said simply, 'but there just isn't time to work anything out. It's touch-and-go whether I win or The Miser wins. I can't take chances, and I shall have to lock you in——'

She nodded, and, opening the door of her room took a key from a drawer in the dressing table.

'It's the only one I have,' she said. 'Father has one.'

Quinion smiled, and for a moment her small hand was gripped in his. Mad though it was, Quinion felt a surge of relief go through him; he was confident that she would be able to explain all that there was to explain, later on.

'Thank you, Gretta.'

He closed the door quickly and locked it, dropped the key into his pocket, and held, in its place, his automatic. For a moment as he walked towards the unknown the smile lingered on his lips, and the sight of the wonderful hazel eyes of the girl was in front of his mind's eye.

The first twenty yards of the passage was familiar, but when he had passed the door through which he had gone on his first visit below the Café, he looked about him more carefully. The lights, which had hitherto been bright, were dim now; only one lamp in every three was alight. It was no handicap, and he pressed on warily, his ears cocked for the faintest sound. He felt uneasy at the uncanny silence which surrounded him; it seemed almost as if the place was empty; yet less than twenty minutes before he had heard Arnold Alleyn's voice, and the footsteps of at least four men.

His breathing was unconsciously stifled. He felt as though he was walking on the edge of a precipice, and that the slightest sound would make him slip and send him falling hopelessly towards eternity, not only for him, but for the world; even the butt of his revolver, gripped firmly in his right hand, gave little comfort.

The passage turned several times and he had walked perhaps fifty yards in all, when he saw a door directly ahead of him. His chin went outwards aggressively; it was now or never. . . . The handle of the door turned at his touch and the door yielded. . . .

Quinion had met with many surprises during the course of his investigations for Department 'Z'. Many of them had been gruesome, most dangerous, and some colossal; but as he saw the contents of that room his blood ran cold. . . .

A dim red glow of diffused light spread downwards from the ceiling, and made the ghastly sight more full of awful fascination. It put each still, silent figure into horrible relief, creating an appearance of blood-red bones.

For round all four walls, with two gaps in front of the doors, two rows of grinning skeletons were sitting on wooden benches. . . .

24

A TALK WITH THE MISER

IT took Quinion a full minute to recover from the shock of that ghastly sight. He felt that the breath had been knocked out of him, and a clammy hand of horror seemed to crawl across his stomach, turning him sick. Ice-cold needles of fear darted into his back alternately with red-hot jabs that might have been of flame. He felt chilled. His blood might have been water for all the strength that he had in his limbs.

Then a maniacal laugh echoed and re-echoed through the room, one moment plaintive, like the moan of a banshee, the next shrill, like the call of a hyena; it fell on Quinion's straining ears like a laugh from the devil himself.

Its effect on him, however, was the exact opposite to that which might have been expected and which was, in all likelihood, intended. It restored his lost realization of the need for action, and without another second's hesitation he stepped towards the door opposite that through which he had come.

He was barely half way across when it opened.

For the second time Quinion found himself face to face with The Death Miser.

Not in his wildest dreams had he expected to meet The Miser by himself; still less had he anticipated an opportunity for taking careful aim at the man whose vast mind had conceived a plot which was to reduce the governments of nations to impotency, forcing them to war against each other for the sake of their very existence. His mind worked like lightning even as he pointed his revolver towards the forehead of The Miser.

The latter's voice, soft and strangely familiar, broke the silence which had lasted from the moment of his appearance.

'I think you will be ill advised to shoot, Mr. Quinn.'

There was a quality in the voice which made Quinion hesitate. He realized that it was probably the reaction after the nightmare moments which had passed. A repetition of that maniacal laugh, a manifestation of anything supernatural from The Miser, or a continued silence would all have strengthened his resolve to shoot; but the voice, evil though it was, struck a different note from the surroundings. Quinion's finger touched the trigger, but did not press it. His voice was calm.

'Why not?'

'Because,' answered The Miser, 'my Council is awaiting the signal to send instructions for immediate action to every country; and the signal is the firing of a revolver.'

The nightmare figure of the man in front of him did not move. The parchment-like face, illuminated by the unearthly red glow, took on a diabolic appearance strangely incongruous when compared with that soft, compelling voice. The crazy crown of a death's head seemed to grin challengingly.

'And I do not lie, Mr. Quinn.'

It was somehow incredible that The Miser would take the trouble to lie; yet Quinion realized that his advantage was slipping away; it was a matter of time, and time only, before someone came to The Miser's aid; then he felt sick as he realized that his coming could not have been unexpected, or at least, not unobserved; otherwise that crazy laugh would not have been sent echoing through the room. With a feeling of sheer dismay that he had never before experienced, Quinion realized that the only person who had known of his presence below the Café was Margaret Alleyn; he had been a thousand times a fool to think that there was no means of communication between the dressing room and the other rooms. A thousand times a fool to rely on the woman whom he knew to be a dupe.

He thrust all thought of Margaret Alleyn behind him; the need was for immediate action and his personal emotions had to be pushed aside.

'Well, I think it's well worth a chance,' he said.

For a second time his finger touched the trigger and for a second time he wavered. For the man in front of him was speaking in that soft, compelling voice.

'As you fire, Mr. Quinn, you destroy every chance of succeeding in your mission; *every* chance. Yet if you neglect this opportunity to destroy me, you retain some hopes of success.'

Once more Quinion told himself that it was crazy, and that his only possible course was to shoot the other where he stood. Yet . . .

'Just how do you mean?' he demanded.

The Miser's voice remained expressionless, and the wrinkled face was immobile, but Quinion had a ridiculous fancy that the other was grinning at him.

'That sounds more as though you are amenable to reason. We shall have to talk. Just one moment. Standing within two yards of your back are two men; they have been there since I first entered this chamber, and at a sign from me they would have killed you.' The Miser broke off for a second, and once again Quinion felt convinced that beneath the parchment-like make-up the man was smiling. 'They still will, if necessary. You would not have pulled your trigger, Mr. Quinn, or at least, you would not have hit me, and you would have necessarily ruined your own prospects. Now, however . . .'

'Granting the two thugs at the back,' said Quinion, breaking in, 'just what are you driving at, Mephisto?'

This time there was no doubting the smile that hovered on the other's lips, and a dozen more wrinkles added themselves to the myriads on that death-like face.

'You have imagination,' said The Miser. 'I would like to drive a bargain.'

Quinion's body tensed. Here was a possible explanation of the other's behaviour, and one that was quite likely true. He was not disturbed by the make-up of The Miser; its object was undoubtedly to frighten, just as the grinning rows of red-hued skeletons were calculated to strike fear into any man. Shorn of all trappings, The Miser was a man who sought power; but, being a man, he placed his personal safety above any other consideration. In spite of his fears for the putting into operation of the vast schemes, Quinion had known that The Miser, and the others of the Council, must have realized that their chances of success had lessened considerably since Oak Cottage had been discovered as a rendezvous, and Cross Farm had been raided. The third set-back—being the fact of his, Quinion's, appearance below the Café of Clouds and the escape of Reginald Chane, must have made them realize that their chances of getting away from the police were small; and, robbed of their freedom, the plans which they had carefully prepared would be useless.

Quinion was fully prepared to believe that The Miser was ready to bargain with him . . . and he was equally ready to respond; time, and time alone, was all that he needed; Department 'Z' would do the rest.

'All right, he said. 'I'm willing to try it out.'

For the first time the man in front of him moved his head. The Miser nodded gravely, and with a satisfaction which Quinion sensed rather than saw.

'I think it will be best if we can make ourselves more comfortable.'

Quinion was glad to be out of that room of death. Afterwards he would investigate those grinning skeletons, and discover whether they were actually the bones of dead men, or whether they were part of some macabre joke on the part of The Miser.

As he passed through that horrible room by way of a small ante-chamber Quinion felt himself go cold. Those two rows of unearthly red bones, imprinted on his mind more clearly now than they had been when he had been face to face with the other man, seemed to have a deeper significance. When he had been at the meeting at Cross Farm he had heard The Miser speak of death. The words seemed to leap in front of his eyes, and for a moment he lived in the past, in the moment when he had first heard The Miser talk of his plans. He had spoken of death, the death of peace and goodwill, to be achieved by the slaughter of innocents. . . .

The voice, which he had likened crazily to death itself, seemed to echo in his ears.

'I have hoarded that death throughout my life, scheming, planning, praying for it. . . .'

Quinion shuddered involuntarily. The word 'hoarded' possessed a ghastly significance; that room, with its terrible hoard of the bones of dead men—and The Miser—The Death Miser——

Only the presence of the two men behind him, whom he could see from the corners of his eyes, stopped him from making one effort to end the whole mad business, to shoot the fearful creature in front of him and be damned to the consequences. In some strange way the men at his back made him realize the vastness of those consequences; he must wait, must play for time, must use every twist of ingenuity that he could control to thwart The Miser.

The latter opened a door and stood back for Quinion to enter. A second later the Hon. James cursed himself aloud for falling so easily into the trap. . . .

Bound fast to a wooden arm-chair was Peter de Lorne; and round him the members of the fearful World Council sat in sinister silence, their crowns of grinning death's heads adding to the horror of the moment.

25

THE MISER ACTS

QUINION made a tremendous effort to recover the control which he all but lost at the moment of his discovery. At the back of his mind one thought and one only drummed incessantly. He must hold out—he must play for time. Time alone could give him a chance of defeating the plans of this macabre Council which aimed at the ruination of the world. The fact that de Lorne had not managed to get away from the Café made the need more imperative, for Quinion imagined that The Miser would feel more secure with both de Lorne and himself helpless in his hands—and in spite of his predicament the agent of Department 'Z' clung to the thin hope that he would be able to escape. If only he could get two minutes at a telephone.

His expression gave no clue to his thoughts, and he made no struggle as the two men who had been behind him gripped his arms and took his revolver from his fingers. Only the flecked grey eyes seemed cold and deadly.

The corners of his lips turned downwards in an ironic grin as he looked at de Lorne.

'Hallo, Peter! You here too?'

De Lorne, after his first momentary sickness of disappointment, recovered himself and grinned back.

'All ready for the party, and you can take it from me that this crowd have any bunch of pierrots whacked hollow. The only trouble is the "no smoking" rule. . . .'

Quinion turned his head slowly and looked at The Miser, who was walking slowly towards the chair at the head of the table round which the Council sat. His progress was halting, and strangely hesitant; Quinion remembered the way in which the man had walked down the stairs at Cross Farm, and was puzzled, for The Miser had given no sign of infirmity when he had burst into the room which hoarded death. A second later the Hon. James experienced yet again the chilling sensation which accompanied the ghastly happenings that had followed in the wake of his first meeting with Thomas Loder.

The eyes of The Miser were turning red!

Quinion swallowed hard and kept his teeth firmly clenched as he watched the man reach his chair and sit down slowly and laboriously. Ten minutes before The Miser, in spite of his parchment-like face, might have been a man in his late forties; now he was moving as a man would who was well past his allotted span, and in whom age had wreaked a terrible vengeance.

Suddenly Simon Hessley's smooth, pleasing voice broke the silence. It was a voice which had moved mass meetings to high pitches of enthusiasm, and there was no doubting the power of the man behind it; at that moment he seemed to dominate even the frail-looking leader of the Council.

'Don't you think, Miser, that the bodyguard is unnecessary now? And couldn't our guests smoke?'

Quinion's lips curled at the other's words, but he was grateful as The Miser spoke in that mellow, aristocratic voice which still held a suggestion of familiarity that the Hon. James could trace, now, as being of the same timbre as Arnold Alleyn's; and Alleyn, he noticed with satisfaction, was not there—unless he was The Miser himself. Quinion's convictions in that direction became firmer; had he not seen The Miser's eyes turn from grey to red in the space of minutes? A second later he felt misgivings which he brushed aside; he had seen those eyes turn red, but had not seen whether they had been grey or blue; the dim red glow of the room which held that grisly hoard had not allowed him to see.

'You are right, Hessley. The men can go. Our . . . guests . . . may smoke too.'

There was no mistaking the fatigue in the man's manner. It seemed to Quinion that The Miser was recovering from a considerable physical effort, and that he was speaking as one would who has been put to sudden exertion.

It was the moment that mattered, however. Had The Miser been no stronger than a child, the presence of the rest of the Council prevented Quinion from acting, and he sufficed himself by taking his case from his pocket and putting a cigarette between de Lorne's lips. Then, still without speaking, he struck a match. He bent low over his friend as the stick flared up. His lips scarcely moved.

'Did Chane get away?' he demanded.

Only de Lorne heard the muttered words, and he responded with a barely perceptible nod. Quinion stood back, considerably relieved. Badly hurt though he was, Chane provided the only link with Department 'Z' that existed. For a moment Quinion's mind was filled with one hope.

He was jerked back to the moment quickly as The Miser spoke again. This time his voice was stronger and the red eyes flamed. The Hon. James darted a quick glance round the table, and saw the grim faces of the twelve men. Kretterlin the Russian was there, Tunn, the Scotsman, Martin Asterling, Hatterson, and Brundt, the German, together with those whom Quinion did not recognize.

The whole Council was ready. And with one stroke they could be made useless! If Department 'Z' did get through, the whole plot would end in failure. If . . .

Quinion groaned at the awful significance of that little word.

'Mr. Quinn'—The Miser's eyes were fixed on Quinion's, flaming red and possessed of tremendous purpose— 'I told you that I wanted to drive a bargain.'

Quinion eyed him calmly and nodded.

'Yes,' he said coolly. 'You lied. . . .'

'I do not lie!' The words spat out, and for the first time Quinion realized one of the great weaknesses in his adversary's mind. Whatever else, The Miser possessed a tremendous vanity, and Quinion made a mental resolve to take advantage of it to the limit. There was no object in forcing the point, however, and he waited as the other went on:

'My bargain is a simple one. Aided by good fortune you have learned a great deal more of the World Council than it pleases me that you should know. That in itself is not dangerous, for you are, shall I say, innocuous. But I am anxious to know just how much of this information you have passed on.'

'All of it,' interrupted Quinion easily. He puffed a cloud of smoke towards the flaming red eyes, but the man went on as though he had seen nothing of the gesture.

'Of course; it is natural that you should say "all of it"; but I am anxious for the truth, Mr. Quinn, and because of the need for it I am allowing myself to discuss the matter with you. Ordinarily I would just act——'

A chuckle interrupted him, and echoed absurdly through the room. The atmosphere was tense; all eyes and ears had been wide open, listening and looking at the two chief actors in the drama that was being played; and the chuckle broke the tension like a knife cutting across a piece of taut string.

'What-ho!' commented de Lorne. 'Jimmy, he does want to be Larry Olivier!'

Quinion grinned spontaneously, and Simon Hessley's lips curled. Kretterlin growled threateningly, however, and for a moment de Lorne thought that the Russian would strike him. Then the tension fell over the room like a cloak as The Miser went on, heedless of the interruption.

'Mine is a simple bargain, Mr. Quinn. I want to know just how much your superiors know. In return for that I will spare the life of . . .'

The red eyes turned from Quinion's towards the door. The Hon. James, who was still standing near the table unguarded save by the threatening muzzle of the automatic which Hessley was holding ostentatiously in his hand, swung round. He would have leapt forward, but Hessley's warning voice told him that to move would mean death; and he needed time; more desperately than ever he needed time.

Bedecked in the regalia of the Queen of the Clouds was Margaret Alleyn. She stood motionless at the threshold, guarded on either side by the two men who had held Quinion close five minutes before.

For a full minute Quinion stood there, looking at her. Never had the look in her beautiful hazel eyes been more helpless; never had he realized the flawless beauty of her as he did then: never had he known such agony of heart as he did at that moment.

'If you touch her you'll swing higher than any man in England!'

Yet even as he spoke a tremendous hopelessness surged through him. If he moved he would be as good as a dead man, and as useless.

Hessley stood up slowly and walked towards the girl. With a word he dismissed the two men, and the door closed behind them. Still without speaking to Quinion he led her towards a chair which was placed at the end of the table opposite The Miser, but his automatic was pointed unwaveringly at Quinion as he moved.

The latter had eyes only for the girl as she sat down without protest. The spirit seemed to have been taken from her; she was listless, lifeless almost; and her very helplessness made Quinion's rage reach white heat.

Yet, for the time being, he could do nothing.

The Miser waited until Hessley had regained his seat before speaking again, and in his mind, strangely cool and working at top speed, Quinion realized the cleverness of the manner in which Margaret Alleyn's entry had been staged. The Miser was playing on his, Quinion's emotions with a devilish ingenuity, but the fact that it was necessary to strive in such a way to break his nerve proved to the Hon. James that The Miser was afraid. The possibility that Department 'Z' knew of the Café of Clouds as the meeting place of the Council was of vast importance, and even as the would-be despot spoke, Quinion had worked the situation out in his own mind, only to have it confirmed.

'I will not mince matters, Mr. Quinn. The exact position is this:

'Our plans, which you learned at the last meeting, have been complete for some time; only the moment at which to strike has been uncertain, and still is uncertain. Due in all probability to the efforts of men like yourself, fighting uselessly to prolong the duration of world peace, two great Powers are not yet primed well enough to co-operate at the moment. It is a matter of days and days only until this has been rectified, but until every country is ready we are unwilling to display our strength.

'In the event of need, however, we will act now, and only you are in a position to tell us whether it is necessary. If we can rely with some degree of certainty on being able to work without interruption for the next forty-eight hours, then we will be able to move, and every country will be inflamed with the frenzied cries of the populace for war! So——'

The Miser's flaming red eyes, glowing horribly in that parchment-like face, turned slowly from Quinion to Margaret Alleyn. The Hon. James followed the other's gaze, sick at heart; yet even as he did so he wondered subconsciously at the slowness of the man's movements, and the fact The Miser turned his whole head instead of diverting his eyes. The mellow voice went on:

'In order to exert all possible influence, Mr. Quinn, you are to be given five minutes in which to reach a decision on whether or not you will give us the information that we need. Should you give it, then this woman will be freed. Should you decide against . . .'

Once more The Miser paused and once more Quinion felt that the white-heat of his fury would burst all bounds of restraint. His teeth were clenched and his fingers were jammed into the flesh of his palms.

The Miser went on. A trace of harshness broke through the mellowness of his voice, and with it Quinion realized that it sounded still more like Arnold Alleyn's. This fiend was talking of his own daughter!

'Should you decide against, then I shall press this button which you can see beneath my hand. It is an electrical contrivance. As it is pressed so will every official wireless station in the world be rendered useless. Report after report of outrages by one country against another will be broadcast. The world will be incited to war . . . and within an hour of the message at least one whole town will be destroyed completely. *I have arranged it!* At this very moment the whole military resources of one Middle Eastern State are ready for battle because of outrages which you have read of in your papers, and which you have believed to be the result of communist outlawry. *Within an hour the greatest war of the world will have commenced!*

'But that, in any case, is inevitable. For my own convenience I wish to defer the first move for another two or three days, and I can only do that if I am sure of being free from interruption. In order to persuade you to talk, Mr. Quinn, I have also prepared this:

'At the moment that I press this button and deliver the call to arms a current of electricity will pass along the steel arms of the chair on which the . . . woman . . . is sitting. It will shrivel her into nothing! The beauty of which she is so proud will be blackened into bones and the perfume which she uses will change for the odour of burning flesh . . .!'

'You—swine!'

The words forced themselves from Quinion's lips. The whole pent-up emotions which had been consuming him burst out in one fierce blaze of fury which made even The Miser flinch backwards. The flecked grey eyes were aflame with hatred and horror. But the muzzle of Simon Hessley's revolver hovered a foot or two from Quinion's face.

With slow, deliberate movements The Miser drew a watch from his pocket. The silence in the room was so complete that the faint ticking could be heard clearly above the constrained breathing of the men and woman.

Margaret Alleyn was leaning forward in her chair. Her lips were parted, her hazel eyes were opened wide with fear, her breath rose and fell tumultuously. For a moment her gaze rested on The Miser; then she looked towards Quinion. The fear which she had had seemed to go from her. She prevented her voice from trembling with an effort greater than any she had ever been called upon to make.

'Don't speak, Jimmy,' she said. 'He may be . . . bluffing.'

A hundred mad ideas rushed through Quinion's mind, only to be thrust aside as useless. Everything was useless; nothing could save Gretta from death nor the world from a revolution that would bring worse than death to millions of men and women. In his mind's eyes Quinion could see the chaos that would follow on the ultimatum that The Miser had ready to deliver.

The leader of the World Council spoke again, a brief sentence that spelled the end of hope.

'You have four minutes left. . . .'

Quinion measured the distance between himself and The Miser. Three yards . . . he could make it easily enough with one leap . . . providing Hessley's automatic didn't finish him. But what good would it do? One man, unarmed, a woman and another man, bound fast to his chair, were helpless against the numbers in the room. It was . . . hopeless . . .

He forced a smile to his lips as he looked into those beautiful hazel eyes. Above all other emotions at that moment the thought that he had believed her in league with The

Miser sickened him most . . . until it was lost in the revelation of the knowledge that her life to him was more precious than anything in the world. He would give everything that he had to save her . . . yet the only means that he could employ meant sending the whole world into chaos.

'We'll call his bluff,' he said slowly. The effort to smile and to speak calmly was almost too much for him, but he succeeded. 'They can't get way with it, Gretta; they must fail. . . .'

The harsh voice of The Miser broke in, and one more brief sentence brought them nearer eternity.

'You have two minutes left. . . .'

Quinion tried to speak, but his tongue seemed to stick to the roof of his mouth. He smiled, putting every ounce of strength that he had into the effort. The silence was complete, a fearful silence that seemed like the herald of death.

For a second time de Lorne broke the terrible tension with a chuckle which, even if it was more forced, made Quinion realize the brief gap between natural living and the horror of that room. And this time even Kretterlin stared at the bound man with something akin to admiration in his eyes.

'If it's cheer-ho, Jimmy—well, we gave 'em a run for their money. . . .'

Quinion smiled back.

'Don't you worry, Peter; we've run them to earth all right.'

The Miser's red eyes flamed. The hands of the watch went remorselessly towards the last few seconds. Every breath seemed hushed.

Quinion poised himself for a spring. He could not speak, of course, but he could make a final effort to end the life of the fiend who sat in that chair with his hand hovering about that fearful button that would spell death for Margaret Alleyn and chaos for the world. The moment that The Miser spoke again Quinion was prepared to make the effort.

The harsh voice broke the awful silence, and every muscle in Quinion's body was tightened for his spring.

'You have decided?'

Quinion leapt.

Hessley, taken completely unawares, lost his touch on the trigger of his automatic and swore beneath his breath. Kretterlin sprang up, but slipped and fell to the ground. The Miser's blazing red eyes loomed up like two balls of fire into the flecked grey of Quinion's and his fingers lost the button and sought desperately for it. But Quinion's steel-like fingers were fastened round the thin neck, and The Miser's strength oozed from him. He struggled furiously, and had Quinion been fighting coolly he would have wondered at the other's strength. But the only thought in Quinion's mind was to end the life of the monster who was writhing in his grasp.

A dozen hands plucked at his coat and tugged madly to drag him away, but he felt that the strength of a giant was in his muscles. His fingers squeezed with devilish purpose; with a strangled gasp The Miser fell limp and lifeless.

And at the same moment a roar filled the ears of everyone in the room. The walls shook and the door shivered violently on its hinges. The pictures fell and smashed on the floor and the electric light swayed ominously. Then de Lorne's voice raised itself above the commotion joyously.

'They've blown up the Café, Jimmy!'

26

A Chat with Gordon Craigie

QUINION'S mind cleared of its red rage in a flash, and he threw the limp form of The Miser from him. He did not move from the spot, however, for he was bent on keeping any of the members of the World Council from touching that fateful button. He wondered at Simon Hessley's failure to use his automatic, but saw the explanation quickly. Hessley, after the first shock of the explosion, had swung round towards the door and the revolver had been knocked from his grasp as the great figure of Kretterlin had forced by him.

Only Hessley and Brundt seemed to realize the vast importance of the button set in the table. The former moved towards it, eyeing Quinion warily, but the latter lunged forward and caught Hessley's chin with a tremendous punch that sent his man flying backwards. Brundt, following behind the Englishman, was taken off his feet as Hessley hurtled back. Then, for the third time, Peter de Lorne chuckled.

There was no need to force it, this time. The sight of the members of the World Council scurrying through a door opposite that through which Quinion had entered, was ludicrous. With one accord they were flying for their lives; it seemed that with the death of their leader they were helplessly lost, and their minds filled with the one great thought of escape. Tunn and Kretterlin had started a panic, and the manner in which Hessley had been knocked out completed it. In the space of a minute there were only five people in the room. The Miser was lolling back in his chair, the red eyes bulging horribly and his tongue half out of his mouth. Hessley, knocked unconscious by striking his head against the corner of the table as he fell, lay inert. De Lorne watched the Hon. James as the latter bent over the still figure of the girl.

Quinion did not hear the noise of footsteps outside the room until they stopped for a moment and a fist hammered noisily on the panels. He swung round as de Lorne called out briefly:

'Bust the damned thing down.'

There were more footsteps and a consultation outside the door, but before anyone had acted on de Lorne's advice Quinion had stepped across the room and swung it open. He receded a step as the muzzles of three revolvers pointed towards him, only to be lowered as the voice of Gordon Craigie broke the momentary silence.

'Not bad, Number Seven. How's the female of the species?'

Quinion licked his lips for a second before he grinned.

'I'll tell you better,' he said lightly, 'if you'll lend me some smelling salts.'

⚜ ⚜ ⚜

Quinion entered the room which he knew to be the head-quarters of Department 'Z' and smiled across at his Chief, who was sitting back in the leather arm-chair and smoking the inevitable meerschaum.

'Gordon,' he said conversationally, 'I never did like that dressing-gown of yours; if I lend you a fiver will you buy a real one? Yellow with blue spots, like a leopard's, or a nice pale pink. . . .'

'No,' answered Craigie, 'I won't.'

'All right,' Quinion said easily. 'I'll hand you my resignation herewith, and this time you're going to accept it.'

Craigie watched the younger man as he dragged the swivel-chair opposite that of the head of Department 'Z'. The Hon. James was dressed in a perfectly cut lounge suit, and was smoking a Virginia cigarette. The flecked grey eyes were smiling contentedly.

'Serious?' demanded Craigie, lifting the meerschaum from his mouth.

'Dead serious,' responded Quinion. 'As a matter of fact, Gordon, I've postponed my wedding for an hour in order to have this chat with you, and it's going to be expensive, what with a special licence and the cabby ticking the tanners while I'm up here.'

Gordon Craigie shifted his meerschaum from his right hand to his left and stood up slowly. Quinion gripped the other's proffered hand and smiled at the laughing eyes of his Chief.

'One of the reasons why you'll be happy, Jimmy, is that you always move fast. She's a nice girl.'

'If you talk to me like that,' grinned Quinion, 'I'll knock your head off. Without exception she's the finest, pluckiest, loveliest—— well, that'll keep, and I haven't much time.'

He took his pipe from his pocket and stretched a hand out for Craigie's pouch. 'Now you can start talking.'

'You know, of course, that Chane rang me up and told me just what the position was,' Craigie said. 'Or rather Felton did, the man who took Chane to de Lorne's place. And you know that we found the Café of Clouds locked all over the place and that the only way of getting in was to blow it up; it seemed safe enough, because from what Chane said all the rooms that mattered were below ground. Everything worked out perfectly . . . you know that too. The whole shoot of the World Council turned up from a house just behind the Café, and as we had something over a thousand men in the neighbourhood, there wasn't much trouble. There's a door leading from the Café itself to the house, of course, and I gather that it was the regular entrance for the great men.'

'Did you get them all?' demanded Quinion. 'I had hoped to be in at the kill, but——'

'If it eases your conscience,' said Craigie, 'as soon as the doctor—I brought one with me, in case of accident—had brought Miss Alleyn round I told him to dose you; you had the stiffest packet of sleeping stuff in that peg of whisky that you swilled from my flask that I've ever seen; so blame it on to me.'

'I'll grant you I was tired,' Quinion put in. 'Carry on.'

Gordon Craigie hesitated for a few minutes before he continued, but Quinion sat silent. 'Well, you know as much as I do about the Council, and The Miser.'

'*Alias* Arnold Alleyn,' interjected Quinion. 'What a man! . . .'

'So you don't know as much as I do. Arnold Alleyn is alive to-day . . . and he'll probably be shot for high treason with the rest of them.'

'Then who . . .?' The Hon. James was perturbed, and he dropped his pipe. 'Then, who the devil . . .'

'The man named Smith *was The Miser,*' said Craigie evenly. 'I had my doubts about that man, although his story was true enough. Loder did ruin him in Canada, and it wasn't until afterwards that Smith began the organization. He used Loder, but always intended to kill him. That was why he was shot at the Café————'

Quinion had recovered from his surprise, and had begun to draw at his pipe again. He took it from his mouth for a moment, however, to interrupt.

'Shot by whom?' he demanded.

'The real Queen of the Clouds. It went like this, Jimmy. Smith and Alleyn . . . I still don't know their real name . . . were brothers, and they had one trait in common . . . a passionate love of the human voice. Soon after he came to England The Miser, or Smith, married an actress who had got mixed up in an international crime organization. It was that which started Smith off on his World Council idea, together with his brother's, Arnold Alleyn's, association with the more prominent thieves; Alleyn, of course, had been a "fence" for many years. By the way, Jimmy, there's one little thing that might ease your mind a bit. . . .'

'Anything is welcome,' Quinion said sadly.

'The fact,' answered Craigie, 'that Alleyn is not Margaret's father. He adopted her when she was a young-ster, and worked it so that she believed herself to be his daughter; and the reason for the adoption was the fact of Margaret's wonderful voice. Even as a child she was a prod-igy. Occasionally, when The Miser's wife wanted an evening off, Margaret took her place; and on the evening before last, when you saw her at the Café, she had been forced to appear under the threat of seeing you killed. Alleyn had let her catch a glimpse of Chane, who was unrecognizable because of the blood over his face, and had told her that it was you; he's about your build, you know.'

'We are clearing things up,' murmured Quinion. 'Hurry, Gordon; the registrar won't wait.'

'Another item is that Margaret appeared on the stage in small parts occasionally, under orders from her supposed father,' went on Craigie, smiling. 'I don't know why, but Alleyn told me that he liked to see her there; it was probably just a twisted type of vanity, Jimmy. Anyhow, that's all I can tell you about your young woman.'

'What else?' asked Quinion.

'Now that gramophone record business. The Miser made one strict law, and all the men who worked with him were scared of him, with the possible exception of one or two members of the Council, which affected all things that were to happen when he was about. You see, he wanted to keep his identity a close secret, and his make-up was so complicated that he couldn't jump into his part at a moment's notice. In order to warn his satellites of his approach he had gramophone records made of his wife's voice. You can see that his passion for the human voice was inordinate. He connected the gramophone to a switch at the doors of Oak Cottage, Cross Farm, and the Café of Clouds. When it played it was a warning that he had everything under control, and that whatever his men were doing must be dropped until he had given further instructions. To a lesser man it would have spelled failure, but with The Miser it helped to establish the complete command that he had over all the members of his organization.

'Smith followed you up when you visited the Cottage with Chane, and decided that the best thing to do was to let you get away, in order to trail you and discover for whom you were working. He had, naturally, a number of opponents in the underworld, and he was not sure whether you were an agent of a rival crime organization, or of the Department.'

Gordon Craigie paused for a moment, smiling across at his friend, who looked ostentatiously at his watch.

'All right,' Craigie conceded, 'I'll be as brief as I can. You know, of course, that Oak Cottage was little more than an exit from Cross Farm. The cottage itself was a mass of sliding doors and movable walls and floors, built by the men who lived at the farm, and when Smith, or The Miser, realized that it was no longer a safe rendezvous, he burned it down.'

Once again he paused, took his meerschaum from his mouth and pointed its long stem towards the other man.

'Which brings us to the two most remarkable things about the whole affair. In the first place, why did he let you raid Cross Farm and get away with your stunt with the whisky and brandy? On the surface it seems crazy that you could have been in the same room as him without being recognized. But . . .' Craigie was speaking slowly but with considerable emphasis, and Quinion waited on his words. The affair at Cross Farm had been inexplicable. . . . 'one thing went wrong which he had not imagined possible,' went on Craigie. 'I've been down to the farm and made a complete investigation there, with the result that I discovered a complicated network of wires which showed on a dial in The Miser's room the exact whereabouts of everyone in the place. Hessley . . . I've been talking with him this morning . . . assures me that the dial told The Miser that you and de Lorne were in the first room into which you broke all the time; the mechanism went wrong, and so did The Miser's plans in consequence.

'The other thing, the fact that he didn't recognize you, was a result of the drug which he took to make his eyes change colour. With his eyes red, the man was practically blind. . . .'

'So that's it,' broke in Quinion. 'That accounts for him looking and walking like an old man. . . .'

'The whole reason,' affirmed Craigie quietly. 'He took the drug purely as a drug . . . *teteni* is the name of it . . . and decided that its effect on his eyes made him more impressive at the Council, and helped him to conceal his identity. And actually it proved his undoing. A queer business.'

'I could find other names,' Quinion assured him. 'But what about the "shut-ear" stuff, Gordon?'

Craigie frowned.

'Frankly, I don't know. The Research Department is taking it up, and there were several phials of stuff at Cross Farm that they are working on. The only thing I know about it is that it works.'

'Thanks,' put in Quinion drily. 'I had an idea that it did.'

The chief of Department 'Z' went on quietly.

'There's only one other thing, Jimmy, and that's pretty horrible. You remember those skeletons at the Café?'

Quinion grimaced.

'They make one of the nastiest pictures I've seen,' he said quietly. 'Why? . . .'

'They were real,' answered Craigie. 'Forty-four skeletons, five of them women.' He was quiet for a moment, then went on grimly. 'Everyone he imagined to be dangerous The Miser killed, and for some macabre reason built up a hoard of death. You did a good day's work when you strangled him, James.' He stood up slowly and put his hand on Quinion's shoulder. 'In fact, it's safe enough to say that you saved everything that's worth saving.'

Quinion grinned awkwardly.

'Tommy-rot!' he said briefly. 'It's all in the game, and, anyhow, the others weighed in as much as I.' He recovered his *sang froid* with an effort. 'Well, I'm sorry I'm leaving the Department. If you should happen to have a little job at any time that a married man could manage. . . .'

Craigie shook his head.

'No, Jimmy. Department "Z's" a home for bachelors with a suicidal turn of mind.'

'I suppose you're right,' acknowledged the Hon. James, smiling reflectively, 'and I've something less than thirty minutes of bachelordom remaining.'

The Chief of Department 'Z' took his proffered hand and gripped it.

'You're a lucky chap,' he said evenly. 'I could say more, but . . .'

'The registrar won't wait,' said Quinion. 'Cheer-ho, Gordon! . . .'

'When you get back to earth,' said Craigie, smiling, 'I'll look in at your cottage. And don't forget——'

'Forget what?'

'That bachelors,' answered Craigie, chuckling, 'make the best godfathers!'

Which remark may have accounted for the difficulty that the Hon. James Quinion experienced half an hour later in slipping a circlet of gold on to Margaret Alleyn's finger.

Redhead

John Creasey

Chapter 1

Martin Storm is Annoyed

The two men lolling against the white rails of the *Hoveric* and gazing dreamily across a widening expanse of water to a grey smudge which an hour before had been easily recognisable as Cherbourg, might well have been mistaken for brothers. Both possessed dark hair, blue eyes flecked with grey, pleasing, irregular features and a physical springiness that even in repose was notable.

There was one physical difference between them, however. Martin Annersley Storm, popularly known as Windy, was two inches taller and proportionately larger than Robert Montgomery Grimm, as popularly called Grimy. In point of fact they were cousins, and if a stranger had overheard parts of their conversation during their lighter moments he might have been forgiven for imagining that their greatest aim in life was to see the last of each other in the least possible time. Nothing could have been farther from the truth.

As they basked in the warm sun they were acutely aware of two things.

Primarily, that the first class sports deck on which they lolled was a vast improvement on the third class steerage which had sheltered them during the voyage from New York to Cherbourg.

The second, that the man with the flaming red hair who was absorbing most of their attention, was extremely popular.

As they looked on, Ginger was performing prodigious feats of strength with a twenty-eight pound iron ball and a vaulting horse brought from the gymnasium for his especial benefit. The point which vaguely annoyed both Storm and Grimm was the revolting enjoyment which he derived from basking in the adulation of an admiring crowd.

After twenty minutes of watching this untiring behaviour, Storm took his pipe from his mouth and remarked mildly;

'Uppish cove, the Ginger bloke.'

'I'd like to poke him one,' Grimm muttered, and from this comparatively long speech Storm knew that the spark of dislike which Ginger had ignited in his own breast had a fellow in Roger Grimm's.

The mutual love of Martin Storm and Roger Grimm for a beano had come within an ace of proving fatal during their stay in New York. A casual, and rather contemptuous reference to 'gangsters' had been taken amiss.

Seven days before embarking on the *Hoveric* they were halfway along a comparatively quiet road from Manhattan to Long Island when something went wrong with their engine.

Then a bullet smashed through the windscreen, cracking against the coachwork, setting up little spurts of dust in the dry road and whirling the startled Storm's hat high into the air. After the first second of stupefaction Storm, crouching low, bellowed a warning to Grimm and drove recklessly into some trees at the side of the road. Like a reluctant turtle the Packard heeled on one side before crashing into the trees. Beneath it, sandwiched tighter than any sardines but much more lively, Storm and Grimm crouched, helpless but fluent.

Though Grimm had recently won a much prized trophy downtown from a world famous heavyweight, all the boxing skill in the world would have been useless against the fusillade from the machine-gun which was being fired from a stationary car twenty yards ahead, and after an interminable barrage they heard the cessation of the deadly tap-tap-tap with heartfelt relief. But they were chalking something up against the gentry; if they had known where it was going to lead them they would have chalked still more furiously.

There followed, after rescue by a passing motorist and a small army of police which had appeared with surprising celerity, a somewhat hectic interview between Storm, as the spokesman of the cousins, and Superintendent O'Halloran of the New York Police. O'Halloran, a big, bluff man with close Irish Republican connections and a carefully nurtured dislike of all Englishmen who didn't drop their aitches, was talkative but unhelpful.

'Sure,' he admitted, 'the bhoys that tried to get ye got away wid it. What wud ye expect? But we've an idea who they were, Mr Storm, don't ye worry.'

'I'm not worrying,' said Storm grimly. 'But it seems to me that you should be. Who was it? And what was the complaint?'

O'Halloran played irritatingly with a petrol lighter.

'As for who it was, Mr Storm, it'd be bad cess to the man as gave them a name without being sure! As for why they picked ye out –'

With an unpleasant grin splitting his thick features he shifted an untidy heap of papers and pulled out a column from *The Courier* which had been cut from a recent issue. After the historic fight which had robbed America of the prized boxing trophy Grimm was a nine days' wonder, and the newspapers' eulogies included Martin Storm. Both had suffered one interview with the Press. One bright spark –*The Courier's* man – had demanded their views on the gangster problem.

And on the following morning a thousand word story was splashed on the front page, which story Superintendent O'Halloran was now fingering.

It ran:

BOXING ENGLISHMEN'S CHALLENGE TO GANGS
'LET 'EM ALL COME' SAYS MARTIN STORM.

ROGER GRIMM, NEW CHAMP, JUST GRINS

The Courier in an exclusive interview with the famous English amateur boxing giants who have just staggered America, Martin Storm and Roger Grimm, learned that neither of these wonderful fighters gives much heed to the gangster menace. 'In England' says Mr Storm, 'we put them where they belong – in jail, with the rest of the small rogues and pick-pockets who prey on humanity. If they show fight – well, what've we got fists for?'

He had said nothing of the kind. But a protest would have brought the whole of the popular Press squealing about their ears, and they had had far too much publicity already; the notice was allowed to pass without complaint.

Storm kept cool with difficulty as he eyed O'Halloran.

'No one took any notice of that tripe, did they?'

'Well, Mr Storm – ' O'Halloran lit a cigar, half-closing his eyes as he leaned back in his chair and rolling the 'Mr Storm' with a calculated insult perfected only by the less pleasant type of Irishman. 'What else wud ye expect? Ye hit them on the raw and they hit ye back.' He opened his eyes suddenly, leaning forward and pushing the cigar an inch from Storm's nose. 'Take it from me, and get away while ye can. Ye're lucky to be alive, an' it's me that says so! Meanwhile ye can rest in peace, for I'm looking after ye.'

Storm rose furiously to his feet.

'Steady,' cautioned Grimm, knowing Storm's happy knack of kicking up a first-rate shindy. 'Leave it, old boy.'

That Grimm's counsel prevailed had no beneficial effect on Storm's frame of mind as he strode along Broadway. It was an unfortunate initial experience of the American police, and his views on that excellent but sorely tried body of men would probably have been even fiercer had he known that several tough-looking hobos lurching behind and in front of him were plainclothes members of the force keeping a sharp eye open for any possible 'accident'.

Less than an hour afterwards, sitting opposite Grimm at the Forty Club, a paragraph in *The Courier* caught his eye. With a snort he handed the paper to his cousin. Grimm read on with tightening lips.

ANOTHER GANG WAR?

A private car whose owner is unknown was fired on and overturned on the Baldwin, Long Island road late this morning. The occupants escaped but avoided the police, who are ignorant of their identity. It seems that this is a fresh outbreak of warfare between rival gangs . . . .

'Ump,' he commented. 'Funny.'

Storm scowled.

'Funny's one way of putting it,' he admitted. 'It at least makes it clear that O'Halloran doesn't want the Press to know who the occupants of the car were. Ask yourself, Roger, why shouldn't the whole world know? No reason at all, unless it's to save us from publicity, which is bunk! No – that dear little Superintendent wants to push us out of the country with little fuss and less Press notice. He doesn't want any shindy kicked up about this afternoon's little wallop. That's plain enough, isn't it?'

'Vaguely,' Grimm admitted. 'But what's the idea?'

'That,' said Storm with some annoyance, 'is the kind of dam' fool question you would ask. Because I can't answer it. But I can tell you one thing. O'Halloran is in for the surprise of his life if he thinks we'll take the hint.' He jerked Grimm's elbow. 'Start moving, my lad!'

'Where to?' demanded Grimm with excusable curiosity. 'Besides, I want another drink.'

'You can want on,' said Storm. 'We're going to have a chat with the bonny boys of *The Courier*.'

Twenty minutes later he was agreeably surprised at the news editor's almost effusive greeting. They were put in charge of a harassed man in shirt-sleeves, who cocked a knowing eye when he heard their names and conducted them through a maze of tables in a vast office. Two dozen men and half-a-dozen stenographers were talking at the same time, bellowing from one end of the room to the other through efficient-looking telephones. Bedlam, in comparison, would have been heaven. Through it all the incessant tapping of typewriters and the perpetual buzz of telephone bells, gave a tenor to the bass-toned roar filling the main office until even Storm and Grimm began to feel thick-headed.

Their escort banged on a door marked:

Geo. Warren – Chief Ed.

and flung it open before the last knock stopped echoing. All three were halfway in the room when the Chief Editor glared up from one telephone and jerked the receiver off another.

Swarthy, unshaven for at least two days, beetle-browed, the massive Chief Editor of the hottest tabloid paper in New York was rasping into the telephone a series of cannon-ball orders which streamed with fluent profanity.

He finished with one telephone and rapped 'keep it' into the other before swerving round on the newcomers.

'Yep?'

Their escort pointed unnecessarily to Storm and Grimm.

'Dem boxing guys, Boss.'

Warren just glared ferociously at the Englishmen, then smiled with sudden and surprising geniality. He pressed a button on his switchboard.

'Keep all my calls,' he rapped.

As the Chief Editor pushed the telephone away from him, cleared a mass of papers, and, with a celerity telling of long practice, revealed a bottle, three glasses and a box of powerful-looking cigars, he leaned back and spoke with the soft intonation of a Southern burr:

'Sit down, gentlemen. Cigars, or smoke your own dope. Drink's comin'. What kin I do for you?'

Storm sat down obediently.

'I don't know – yet,' he admitted cautiously.

Warren began pouring drinks.

'Well, maybe it's that li'l story we wrote up, Mr Storm. I jus' can't tell you how sorry I am, an' that's the real truth. The guy that wrote that story's getting the biggest takedown he's ever had since his lullaby days, and it won't be my fault if he doesn't write up a full apology! Take it from me he's –'

Storm grinned.

'I'm not worrying about that write-up. It's the little job that followed it I'm after.'

Warren's squat body went taut as he glared up.

'What job?'

Leaning back in his chair, Storm flicked a speck of ash from his perfectly creased trousers.

He said gently: 'You can tell the bright lad who wrote up that pack of lies that we meant all we said and a lot more! Tell him that all the gangsters in the universe wouldn't make us turn a hair! Tell him we've been telephoning the British Ambassador at Washington and that he's kicking up the biggest shindy U.S.A.'s ever thought of! Tell him – ' He leaned forward, tapping the gaping Warren's fleshy shoulder. 'Tell him to put more lies in his write-up than he's ever thought of in his young life, and get you to help him! That ought to do the trick!'

Warren shot him a look of almost panic from beneath his beetling brows.

'What trick?'

Storm grinned engagingly and stretched his legs. There was considerable satisfaction in having tied up the great George Warren, Chief Editor, but too much leg-pull would have made him lose sight of his main objective – that of finding, if possible, why O'Halloran was hostile and who were the likely gunmen behind the outrage of the afternoon. Warren, if he had realised the crazy plan of reprisals formulating in Storm's mind would have gulped: 'Heck!

What innocents!' Neither of the Englishmen had the slightest idea of the deep-rooted fear inspired by the gangster menace, nor of the soulless murder-machinery run by rival racketeers.

'I've just been talking to a lad called O'Halloran at Police Headquarters,' said Storm mildly. 'I don't like O'Halloran and I don't like the way he froze up on that Long Island shooting job this morning.'

Warren's thick lips closed in a straight line. He lost his uncertainty and from his prominent eyes there shone a kind of secondhand but biting fear. His voice was thick.

'Were you in that car?'

'We were,' assented Storm grimly, and showed the hole in his hat.

Warren seemed frozen stiff. Then:

'And you got away with it! Cripes, but you're lucky!'

'O'Halloran suggested that,' murmured Storm.

Warren hardly seemed to hear him. He was staring through, not at, the two Englishmen, and that frightening expression of near-fear sent an irrepressible shiver through their blood.

'That's Redhead!' he rasped hoarsely. 'Only Redhead would have done it! And I thought he was out of the country or I'd 'a cut my fingers off before okaying that story!'

'Nice of you,' Storm murmured, 'but what's it all about? Who's Redhead?'

'He's the deadliest swine we've ever had to contend with. He's got more murders against him than all the others put together. There ain't a racket he's not in somewhere, and there ain't a fly cop can pull him for selling poison liquor. I reckoned he was out of the States, Storm, or I swear I wouldn't have run that story. We've had it before. Dumb guys grinning at the gangs – and it's usually their last grin when Redhead's near. He thinks he's Almighty, and, tarnation, he damn near is!'

There was something compelling about Warren's manner, making Storm and Grimm realise that the newspaper man was giving them the naked truth. To them, imbued with the Englishman's unshakable belief in the superiority of law and order, it seemed impossible. But they were in New York, not London, and the grip of the gangs was tightening round them, monstrous, murderous, filling the very air with ominous threats.

'So that's it, is it? We trod on Redhead's corns and he's after us. And all the police in New York daren't – '

'It ain't daren't!' interrupted Warren, taking a grip on himself. 'It's can't. They think it's him, but they can't be sure – and if they were they wouldn't know who it was, apart from just the name: Redhead. That's all you can get from squealers with the gangs, just Redhead, and it's enough to make a man order his box if Redhead's put him on the spot.' He crashed one great hand into a vast palm. 'I reckon O'Halloran thought you'd really said all those things, Storm, and a man who'd do that asks for trouble. I reckon he wants to get you out of the country fast, because if anything happened to you there'd be a stink with your little island, and we don't want that in U.S.A.'

He pushed back his chair and stood up, pointing the tip of his cigar towards Storm.

'Son, you don't know things over here. You don't know Redhead, and I reckon you want a peck at him. Well, forget it! I wouldn't print your story for all the gold in China! It'd sign your death warrant. Swallow your pride and get out of here while you can. Don't go first class. Travel third, like a couple of bohunks, and don't show your noses out on the first class deck until you've reached Cherbourg.'

He shot out a hand, gripping Storm's.

'Say! I could shoot myself for printing that story, but I'm right glad to've seen ye both. But the yarn went round that Redhead was halfway across the Atlantic, and things were kinda dull. I'm darn sorry. I'll print a headliner, saying it was all bunk, though if Redhead's after you a headliner won't help. I'll put a coupla men to keep an eye on you, and I reckon O'Halloran's watching, too.'

He looked sombre.

'And don't argue, you guys. Believe me, if you don't get out damn quick you'll be stone cold in no time at all, and I kinda don't want your shooting up on my conscience, see? Come an' see us again, when things are quieter. All right? G'bye.'

Love John Creasey?

Get your next classic Creasey thriller for FREE

If you sign up today, you'll get all of these benefits:

1. Complimentary ebook of REDHEAD (usual price £2.99)

2. Details of the new editions of his classic novels and the chance to get copies in advance of publication, and

3. The chance to win exclusive prizes in regular competitions.

Interested? It takes less than a minute to sign up. You can get the novel and your first exclusive newsletter by visiting www.johncreaseybooks.com_

CPSIA information can be obtained
at www.ICGtesting.com
Printed in the USA
LVOW07s0157220617
538957LV00001B/131/P